The Tales of John Kneebone
As Collected By
John Wearne
Churchwarden and Overseer of the Poor
Wendron Parish
Cornwall

In Memory of Susan Pellowe

MYRGH PELLOWE

(See what you made me do?)

'The Tales of John Kneebone' is a collection of stories. These stories were written by several authors, each in their own unique and inimitable style.

These stories are intended to entertain.

This is not a history textbook, and may contain speculation, interpretation, paradox, anachronism, catachresis, invention, errata, corrigenda, hyperbole, ambages, erethism, amphigory, palilogy and even roman a clef.

These are included at no extra charge.

Contents

Introduction

My name is John Wearne. I am a Churchwarden of the Parish of Wendron in the Duchy of Cornwall. Realizing that such a statement is unlikely to arouse in the reader a fervent interest, I will hasten to say that this book is not about me.

Just whom this book is about, and details of the character (rather — lack thereof!) of the person who is the true and rightful subject of these tales will be revealed in due course. I am not a droll-teller, but a man of business and of some means, and am used to stating a matter in its proper form with a beginning, a middle and an end, and with a minimum of romancing.

I attained my threescore years and ten only this last October. My family is long-lived, and, as I am in reasonable health, I make bold to tempt Providence by stating a wish that I may tarry a while yet. I hold no hope of seeing the dawn of the New Century – the 19th since the Birth of our Dear Saviour. Dear me – what a frame such a thought puts around one's soul. Our mortal selves are finite, after all.

I have been, as I believe I mentioned, and continue to be, a Churchwarden. I thank God that I have been so honoured by my neighbours and fellow-parishioners of Wendron Church for many years. Since my income derives from property and private investments, I am not constrained to keep hours at an office, court, counting-house or surgery as are many men of my station. Therefore I am more at liberty to discharge the duties of Warden without interference from the daily demands of a livelihood.

The duties of Churchwarden are many. This is especially true in our little (though very ancient and august) parish in that the office of Warden comprises also the office of Overseer of the Poor. I help, of course, to manage the affairs of the Parish Church itself, what little management that calls for. We see to our affairs, and the affairs of our Mission in Helston, well enough during our occasional meetings and incidental discussions. Our Vicar is a capable man and is able to deal with daily upkeep and arrangements of the Church itself, with the help of steadfast and energetic parishioners.

It is in the discharge of my duties as Overseer that I am privileged to come in contact with a more varied and colourful, if also a more squalid and pungent sector of our district than I might otherwise do.

I say 'privileged' with a touch of irony, of course. I am not a fastidious man, nor a prig or a prude. I have seen much in my time, and have raised a family and have grandchildren, with all that that brings, both joyful and sorrowful. I have served as an Officer (a very junior one) in the Army (well – the local militia) and have seen violent death and maimed bodies.

Therefore my duties as overseer which include being present at births and deaths, holding the hands of the indigent sick as they cough themselves well or dead in the workhouse, dandling soiled babies on my knee as their mothers stand trial for theft and worse, assisting nauseated, incontinent, drunken men (and women!) to their doors are not as much a matter of shock, distaste and disillusionment to me as they might be to some others.

One of my charges, indeed, became (although it would have done no good for me had he known it) something of a pet of mine. I say 'became' in the past tense as he has been gone from the Parish for some years now.

He was a man of little worth. Where he came from, I have never determined. He was not born in the Parish, but drifted in during his young days, barely old enough to be outside of a family circle. He was so capable of seeing to himself and living by his wits that I wonder if he ever knew a mother and father, or if he was raised wild, by the badgers and foxes.

I often would, as he grew to manhood, encounter him in my Official Person, it being my task, sometimes, to convey those arrested for petty crimes to trial and to prison to serve their terms when convicted. We became quite well-acquainted in many of such journeys. He eventually married, Lord help his poor wife, and had sons of his own. Not that he showed a speck of feeling toward them other than to, when out of gaol, stop in to see them in their miserable hovel – or in the workhouse, sometimes – and bring them a coin or two.

This person was in most ways no different from the dozens of human dregs which pestered me and took up my time in dealing with their crimes and poverty. He did, however, possess something – a spark – which set him apart.

I often encountered him in a certain sort of situation. In such, he would have gained the ear of someone, or some several persons, with his gift, which was for entertaining talk.

Once he had ingratiated himself, he would tell stories. These stories, most of which I knew of my own knowledge to be untrue, had one purpose: to wheedle and extract from the listener a bit of coin, a drink or some other gain. The stories always shared two attributes. They were lies, tailored to fit the listener, and they were in answer to the question 'How did you lose your leg?'

He was a one-legged man, and his name was John Kneebone. In this book, I hope to record some of his stories. The 'Tales of John Kneebone.'

The Sailor's Tale

It was a lovely Summer's evening in Helston. In Coinagehall Street the fading light was soft and subtle. The granite of the grander buildings had a warm glow; the wind was a mere zephyr blowing in from the sunset. There might have been the occasional spot of rain, but it was not really noticeable and anyway it brought a sweet freshness to the air.

I had ridden into town for a venturer's meeting, which would undoubtedly be followed by some pleasant socialising with my old friend James Medhow. He had an uncanny knack for locating the finest Canary, which always helped the evening along. I left my horse at the Anchor Stables but then as I emerged onto the street I saw a disreputable figure approaching. He glanced left and right then slipped surreptitiously inside a nearby kiddlywink.

The figure was dressed a sailor and limped badly. To my concern it looked suspiciously like John Kneebone, a rogue who had mercilessly plagued Wendron and Sithney for as long as I could remember. Last I heard he was on the treadmill in Bodmin Jail, which was probably the best place for him. 'How had he escaped?' I wondered. There would undoubtedly have been some double-dealing involved.

Luckily he did not notice me. Mentally I revised my own plans for the evening to ensure I could avoid him. But as I waited in the street I could not resist moving a little closer to the door of the kiddly and eavesdrop on the conversation inside. I could only hear half of what was said, but it went like this …

Hello? Anyone in? Please can a poor ole sailor come in out the wind an' rain?

Ah, thank 'ee very much, very civil of you. A very kind young lady you are.

Yes, it's a rough ole night isn't it. Appearances can deceive, it's nearly as bad as the Southern Ocean in Winter. It's good to be inside by a nice warm fire when it's so cold and wet outside.

Yes, a specially cosy kiddly, this is. That's what my late faather always said, he did. An' me poor ole mother too, God bless her. Mind you, he now ships with Davey Jones and she passed away this very day one year ago. Terrible sad! Her last words were 'You get into Helston son, and see that nice lass in the kiddly.'

Oh, thank you, yes, a terrible shock and I am gettin' over it, just about. But your sympathy is much appreciated.

I don't suppose you'd mind if I sat by the fire? I only got one leg see, poor ole shellback that I am. Standing up for any length of time is rather difficult. It's hard: some unkind people suggest I'm unsteady on my feet due to the demon drink. It's really cruel when in fact you're sober as a judge, but just struggling to get by every day. Truth is I never touch a drop. 'Cept for medicinal purposes that is.

Thank you kindly, my dear. Yes, another log on the fire would be welcome. Careful how you bend there.

Well now, that is a pretty little chemmy you have on. Shows off your, er, attributes to best advantage. I don't suppose you could spare a nipperkin for a poor old salt, just for 'is bad leg?

Oh well, never mind. I quite understand an' I wouldn't want you to get into trouble. If you don't mind I'll just warm myself for now.

Local maid are ye? Yes, I thought as much, pretty as a peach. You can tell, you know. I always say the prettiest maids come from, where are we?

Yes, that's right. I always say the prettiest maids come from Helston. I know what I'm talking about, I've been all round the world 'tis true: Falmouth, Padstow, Fowey and Looe.

What? Oh, thank you, very generous of you. I'm afraid that these days the ale is my only relief. Poor ole sea dog that I am. Served the King all my life and all I got to show for it is a wooden leg. Constantly wracked with pain I am. Ooh yes, agony it is. They say that shark bites never heal.

Yes, shark. Big fish, with a mouth like a kibble, teeth like razors and a sense of humour like a hangman.

What? Yes, a bit bigger than a pilchard.

Why, don't you believe me? You should trust me, you know. A loyal servant of the King I wuz.

Oh, all right then, seeing as you ask me then I'll tell you the tale.

It happened like this. I shipped aboard the 'Athelstan' out of Fowey. A three-master she was, built on the Gannel. I can promise you it was the worst voyage I was ever on. We were s'posed to be makin' for Hispaniola with a cargo of pianos. At first we made good Westings across the Atlantic. But then we was becalmed something dreadful in the Doldrums. Stuck for days in the Sargasso Sea we wuz. We were there so long that the seaweed moored itself to the hull to save itself the trouble of floating. It was so thick we used to play cricket on it every afternoon. Never once lost a ball.

Then, all of a sudden, a great trade-wind come in from the north west. We only just managed to scramble back on board before it blew us clean out of the weed. Thirty knots of wind there was. Reduced to reefed tops'ls we were, hardly a pocket handkerchief aloft. Sails no bigger than that chemise of your'n, and not half as pretty. The waves, they wuz so tall they blotted out the sun. The ship's sundial didn't work at all. The only way we could use it was by the light of the moon. Twenty-four days it blew with no respite, an' we could neither go port nor starboard, let alone turn back. Six thousand miles we wuz blowed till we sighted land. We'd been blowed right back across the Atlantic Ocean.

Since that day when ever you hear someone say, 'Well I'll be blowed!' then they're talking about me, even if they don't know it.

At last, on the horizon we spied a great flat-topped mountain. It looked like granny's kitchen table it did. The place we arrived at was Kapstadt. Cape Town, it's called in English. Full of Dutchmen it was. I liked them, good sense of 'umour. But you'd never pick a fight with them. They were mighty men, all twelve feet tall. Yes, twice as big as normal 'umans; double-Dutchmen they were. Spoke nothing but double Dutch. It was hard to hear 'em, they were so far up in the sky.

Anyway, we got provisions there an' set off once again. We all had to wear ear plugs on watch, the wind and waves were deafening: that's why it's called the roaring forties.

Then one fateful mornin' the sea-cook reported to the Cap'n, 'It's a 'mergency, not only have we run out of saffron buns, we've run out of pasties.'

So we ate everything edible on board. Yes, desperation is a cruel mistress. The whipping twine they made into spaghetti, the fenders they made into steaks. They chopped up tarred hawser and fried it as sausages. You know they even took Trelawny, my talking parrot from off my shoulder.

I still weep when I think of it. I shall always remember his last words. He said 'Shall Trelawny die?' and the Cook said 'Yes!'

Tasted horrible did Trelawny and the feathers got caught between your teeth, but we lived off parrot stew for a week. Then there was nothin' left to eat at all; it was the moment of truth!

'It's no good,' sez the Cap'n, 'We shall 'ave to eat one of the crew. The men must draw lots to see who we will have for supper.'

So they cut up a load of straws, one for each member of the crew. They carefully trimmed them to the same length, except for one that was cut shorter than all the rest. Then we each had to take a straw from the sheaf.

An' guess who drew the short straw. Yes, it was me. To save me shipmates I was to be killed alive n' made into an 'uman pasty. Sacrificed in the name of Cornish cuisine.

So the cook gets out his steel and starts sharpening his slaughtering knife. They lash me to the mast so I can't resist, and I says a final prayer before they end my life.

I think to myself, 'What a sad fate, to travel the world, to have the body of a Greek god, to have the intellect of a genius, and to end up as the filling for a Cornish pasty.

But then the cook goes, 'Aree-faa! This dirty sea-dog hasn't washed for 40 days. Before we eat him he must have a bath.'

An' the rest of the crew agreed. 'Give 'im a bath,' they all shouted, 'We don't know where he's been.'

'Give him two baths,' said the Bosun, 'I do know where he's been.'

'Right on lads,' sez the Cap'n, 'Make ready to lower the pinnace.'

So they puts me into the dinghy an' they lower it astern o' the ship.

'You git yourself washed boy,' sez the Cap'n, then 'ee chucks me a bar of soap an' a scrubbing brush.

So I thought 'I better do as I'm told. I'll start at the bottom and work up'. I take off my trousers and lower my legs into the sea, then I begin scrubbing 'em with the brush. Then all of a sudden, up pops this monster shark an' he grabs my toes. I mus' be careful not to zaggerate, but he mus' ha' been 40 feet long.

You can be sure I hollered loud and long.

'Hey lads,' I shouted, 'I just caught a giant shark.'

I reached out to try an' grab the shark, but he was very slippery an' most of him was in the water. I could only reach as far as 'is gills and then I could hardly tickle him, let alone offer him violence.

But lucky for me he was a ticklish shark and he doubled up with laughter. So with a mighty effort I grabs him by the tail and drags him into the dinghy. This made him pretty wild I can tell you.

By then he had nibbled his way up to my ankle.

'C'mon lads,' sez I, 'Quick, else your human pasty will be eaten by this gurt, great sea monster. If you're speedy we can all have fish pie instead!'

You can be sure they shinned down the ladder into the dinghy pretty quick.

Well the shark had continued nibbling as best it could and now it had got to my knee. I was starting to get worried about my old John Thomas.

What? Oh, don't worry I'll explain later.

Luckily the first down the ladder wuz the Cook with his great slaughter knife, an' he took off the shark's head with one mighty blow.

Yes, of course sharks 'ave heads. Stands to reason, they gotta have some place to put their ears 'aven't they?

Well the shock made the shark open his jaws a yard wide and take one last great bite. He bit my leg clean off, nearly to the hip, the old rascal.

So they pulled me an' the shark back up the ladder. The surgeon he bandaged up my stump. All of us had fish pie for days on end, an' the officers had shark's fin soup for breakfast.

The ship's carpenter made me a wooden leg out of a spare jib-boom and soon I wuz peggin' around like a good un.

The very next day I was up in the crow's nest when on the horizon I saw clouds, then breakers and sand.

'Land ahoy!' I shouted.

'What did he say,' asked the Ship's Navigator, who was rather deaf.

' 'Land ahoy!' sez the Cap'n.

'Are you sure?' asked the ship's Navigator, 'Tisn't on the chart.'

'Sure as eggs is eggs,' sez I. An' right enough two hours later we arrived at a desert shore. Completely unknown it was, not on any chart at all.

Then the Navigator says, 'This could be dangerous, we don't know the depth of water here.'

So I called the ships carpenter and got him to paint depth marks up my wooden leg, all neatly marked in feet and fathoms. Yes my dear, if you look closely you can still see the marks at the top of my leg. It was such a good idea that to this day you find such markings on the bow of all ships. Not that anyone ever thanked me for it of course.

Then the Cap'n sent me ashore to see if it was safe. I measured the depth with my wooden leg then I scrambled ashore. So there was I peggin' up the beach when I saw these hoof prints in the sand.

'Can you see anything boy?' shouts the Cap'n.

'Just an 'orse trail 'ere,' says I.

'What did 'ee say?' says the Navigator.

'Australia,' sez the Cap'n, so the Navigator wrote it down on the chart.

Anyway then the locals pitched up, so we taught them to drink tea an' play cricket, and they've done that to this very day.

So you see it was me, ole John Kneebone that found Australia. And have I had a word of thanks? Nah, not one!

Oh, thank you, that's very kind of you. Yes, another drop would go down very well.

Well we didn't want to stay for too long in Australia. 'Twas a lovely place, the weather was warm and the people were very friendly, but there wasn't a kiddly near as good as this un, an' the food there was really bad. No pasties at all.

'Send us a decent cook, Cap'n,' said the Australians. So, when we got home we passed that message on. I don't know what the Admiralty intends to do about it. They usually get such things all muddled up.

They called the place where that monster shark bit off my leg the Great Australian Bite. The story must be true 'coz they still call it that to this very day. Tis as true as I'm standin' 'ere.

Do you know, when I got home I found my sweetheart had sold my cottage an' run off with some darn foreigner. Came from Tavistock they say. So now I'm all alone in the world.

I don't suppose you could spare another nipperkin could you?

One Good Turn

In later years which I will touch on before I've done with Kneebone, I encountered several persons, Gentlemen and not, who knew, too well, Kneebone in the days between the time I knew him as a ne'er-do-well in Wendron and the time in which he became…. well, more of that later.

One of those persons had been a young lad at the time he knew Kneebone (by a different name,) a lad to whom Kneebone had, he professed, taken a liking. Several times, that lad had been in a position to help John by influencing the opinions of those who held John's fate in their hands.

I am of the opinion that the following tale was made up out of whole cloth to impress that lad and turn him to Kneebone's side, but I present it as it was written up by that lad, having become a worthy Gentleman (partly, and unintentionally, thanks to Kneebone!)

I say that I present it as written. In fact, I have changed only one thing — in that the name that the lad knew John by was not Kneebone. I have taken the liberty of giving him back his own name. Here's the story (almost) as I received it:

It was another night of the full moon, to light the path for John Kneebone to make his way the mile and a half from his home near Lanteglos to the Stag Inn at Polruan, set near the head of Betty Woon's Steps. A fair distance for a one-legged man, to be sure, but over the decades, Kneebone had become quite agile on the mahogany replacement, and become accustomed to the pressure it exerted on his hip joint. Besides, the exercise kept him hale and hearty, preventing the paunch that bedevilled other men in their mid-forties, and there was always a good welcome, warm fireside, and fine ale to be found at the hostelry run by the affable Jago Uren.

From his comfortable fireside seat, he looked over his almost empty pint pot to catch the eye of the resplendently bearded landlord, who acknowledged the hint with a friendly wink and a smile. The hostelry was moderately busy. More folk would come later in the evening, when the last of the fishing fleet straggled home.

Kneebone looked up sharply as the door opened to admit a stranger, startled by the fact that the room had suddenly fallen silent. The newcomer was a tall, rather shambling, figure of Kneebone's own years, but leaner than he. A thatch of prematurely grey hair, more iron-grey than white, straggled to the man's shoulders, while the clean-shaven face was thin and gaunt, heavy-lined and hollow-cheeked, the face of a man to whom life had been harsh. He wore a patch over his right eye, of crimson rather than the black favoured by other men who'd suffered such a misfortune.

It was not the arrival of the stranger that had caused the sudden silence in the bar, but that of his companion. It was the biggest hound that Kneebone had ever clapped eyes upon. The creature was immense, its shoulders reaching to thigh height on a man, and it padded at the stranger's side with easy obedience. John could not be certain of its breeding; to his eye it suggested a mixture of Irish Wolfhound and Great Dane.

'A pot of your finest, landlord, if you please,' he heard the man say pleasantly to Uren, who also could not take his eyes from the gigantic animal at the stranger's side. 'I give you full assurance that Bosun will be of no trouble to you or your custom. He is well accustomed to fine hostelries, and his conduct in each and every one has been immaculate. I have taken the greatest care with his training, and he as fine a companion as a man such as myself could wish for.'

'Then, sir, both he and your good self are most welcome,' said Uren. 'By your kindness, might I ask that you pass this pot of ale to the gentleman by the fireside while I pour your own? He has but one leg.'

The stranger glanced at Kneebone, and the mahogany leg, and nodded his assent. 'It shall be my pleasure.' Taking the ale, he made his way over to Kneebone but, at this point, the hound spotted the fireside to curl beside, and cut in front of the stranger who stumbled, tipping half of the ale over the table.

'Damn you, Bosun, have a care where you're going, will you?' he grumbled, then to Kneebone. 'My deepest apologies, my good sir. Pray allow me to purchase another pot in payment for this clumsiness.'

Kneebone chuckled. 'No damage done, bar loss of good ale. As you've a civil tongue in your head, I most heartily accept your kind offer. Now that your most magnificent hound has settled himself by the fire beside me, you are most welcome to sit at this table, once Elspeth has mopped up.' He waved a hand at the landlord's wife, bustling forward with cloth in hand. The stranger nodded his thanks and returned to the bar before bringing back fresh pots of ale for himself and for Kneebone.

'Thomas Pearson,' he said, introducing himself and extending a hand that Kneebone shook heartily. 'Assistant to Lord Robartes's estate manager at Lanhydrock. As I also have past maritime experience, his Lordship sent me to meet with Martin Williams, shipping agent at Fowey, to bespeak transport for horses he has purchased in Spain. I took lodgings for the night not far outside this village and shall take the ferry from here in the morning for the appointment. My good hosts recommended this hostelry to me.'

'John Kneebone of Lanteglos,' he reciprocated. 'Netmaker for a good many years. Fishermen from Polruan, Fowey, Polperro and even Looe come to me for new nets, or to repair their damaged ones. A passably gentle trade for a man of my years, and a decent enough living for my meagre purposes.'

Pearson glanced down at the mahogany leg jutting alongside the small table. 'Not the sole trade of your life, I'll be bound. Tell me, John, if the memory does not cause you distress, how you came to such a pass.'

Kneebone leant back and chuckled. 'The price of a misspent youth, Master Pearson. It is no secret hereabouts, and it will do no harm to explain it. I was young then, many years past, and brash enough to be easily drawn into the world of free-trading on a vessel named the *Falcon*, plying the night runs from Polperro to Roscoff. A rare time we'd have over there, I can tell you, as we'd meet up and carouse with free-traders from Plymouth to the Land's End. We'd load up with contraband and bring it ashore at Talland, where the parson turned a blind eye for as long as his baccy and brandy arrived at his door. That is, until the fateful day that we were betrayed.'

'Betrayed, you say?'

Kneebone sighed. 'For whatever reason drove him to it, the *Falcon*'s first mate, one Piers Trevanion, decided to turn King's Evidence on us. A revenue cutter lay in wait one night as we returned with a fresh cargo. She was armed, and we were armed, and the fight was terrible to behold, let alone be part of. A lot of good men died or were maimed that night, on both vessels, and the *Falcon* was sent to the bottom. A handful of us struggled to shore, but my leg was gone and I was dragged ashore by the captain.'

'And yet you live, a free man?'

'With but a single leg, and after five years of hard labour once they finally caught up with me. The captain they hanged at Execution Dock.'

'And what of the man Trevanion?'

'I was informed that he was aboard the Revenue cutter that night, and fought against us to boot, for all the good that it did him. He was captured one night, sometime later, and tried for his free-trading, regardless of his betrayal and service to the Revenue men. Local squires and magistrates who derived much benefit from our trade, insisted upon it. He, too, had his neck stretched on Execution Dock.'

Pearson gestured at Kneebone's mahogany leg. 'You must surely find his conduct a hard matter to forgive.'

'For many years, that was the truth of it.' Kneebone replied. 'Until I met with a man named John Wesley, who taught me the paths that I must tread and of the virtues of forgiveness. So it is that I can finally forgive Piers Trevanion, but his deed is a harder thing to forget.'

It was time to change the subject. Kneebone gestured at the crimson eyepatch. 'And what of yourself, Thomas? You mentioned a maritime past. A ship of the line, I'll be bound.'

Pearson inclined his head. 'You might say that. It was nought more than a skirmish, but a vicious one for all that. I could not have been greatly older than yourself at the time you lost the leg. I was fortunate to keep at least one of my deadlights and find a less hazardous road through life.'

A further hour of pleasant conversation passed, with two more pots apiece of Jago's excellent ale, while the great hound curled peacefully and contentedly at the fireside. Kneebone finished his ale and stood.

'I fear the time has come for the homeward journey,' he said. 'I prefer to be abed before midnight, and I cannot travel as quickly as most men. I go by way of the clifftop track, trusting to the full moon to light my way.'

'Then, by your leave, John Kneebone, Bosun and I shall come part way with you, as the same path will take me to my own lodgings as well as any other. We will be content to travel at your own pace. Who knows? Bosun here may find opportunity to catch rabbits, at which art he is most wonderfully skilled. He pleases Lord Robartes, who is most partial to rabbit stew, and Bosun has a singular way of catching them. He cleanly breaks their necks in his jaws, without as much as breaking the skin, and always brings them back unbloodied. With good fortune, he may find you your morrow's dinner.'

Disappointingly, the hound had found no prey by the time that Pearson and Kneebone had toiled to the highest point of a path well lit by a full moon in a clear sky. Before them, another path led away and inland.

'I shall take my leave of you here, John Kneebone,' said his companion, 'My lodgings are but a short distance away. It has been a most pleasurable meeting, and I thank you for it. You travel surprisingly well on that peg-leg, my friend.'

Kneebone paused as the shambling figure with the huge hound padding silently alongside him half turned so that the moonlight fell upon his face. His breath caught in his throat momentarily. The cold rays seemed to smooth out the ravaged features, provoking memories of a face long forgotten. Surely, it could not be?

The path that his companion had pointed out led only to one place. As far as Kneebone knew, only old man Trevanion lived there, his family gone before their time, their end hastened by the shame that had stained their family name for a brace of decades. He came to a halt, suddenly uncertain.

His mind whirled back in time, staring at the man, envisioning a head of neat dark hair kept short, instead of an unkempt thatch of iron-grey. From a past long gone, he saw again a smooth, confident face, with trim dark beard, unravaged by age and injury. *But this cannot be! Piers Trevanion was executed years ago.*

Turning to face him, the stranger watched his expression of incredulity, and with a smile that was suddenly cruel. 'So, you know me at last, John Kneebone. Execution Dock never witnessed my demise. At the last moment, their Lordships relented and commuted the sentence, remembering the service I had rendered them. Instead, I was transported, far from home, across the ocean to Maryland in the Americas, where their mistake was to put me to work as a shipwright, and even you will remember that I built good boats. The *Falcon* herself was one of those, and she took a fearsome battering that night off Talland before she sank. I was treated well in America for my skill, far better than many of the poor souls who were similarly condemned, but after years I cannot even count, I stole one of the boats that I built, leaving two guards on the sands with their throats slit, and I had deliberately built her sturdy enough to carry me home.

'I sailed her single-handed to Ireland, where none knew me, and where I acquired this faithful hound. There, and for seven long years, I planned my return and revenge. I crossed to Britain to seek out and slay every man jack that survived from the *Falcon* that night. I needed no weapon and require none, for I have Bosun, and he is well trained in more than one art. All but one last man died in his jaws, and that long wait ends this very night. Your time has come, John Kneebone.'

Kneebone stared at his old enemy. 'So it *was* you on the Revenue boat that night. There were others who survived it who claimed so.'

Trevanion allowed himself a grim smile. 'Who do you think cost you that leg? I was commanded to man the swivel gun, and did good service that night. It was your own lucky shot that took my eye, and mine was a reflex action. Not the finest of aims, as it should have killed you outright. But, even with the pain I endured, the one eye that remained saw that it had taken your leg. One good turn deserves another, do you not agree?

'Those of you who survived and made it to shore scattered to the four winds. Doubtless, they got you to a sawbones in time to save your carcass before transporting you to somewhere far from Talland, by boat or by horse and cart. It matters not. Mayhap the Land's End or the Lizard, wild places in which to skulk from discovery.'

'St Keverne, if you have the need to know,' Kneebone answered jauntily, while all the time his mind whirled, seeking a means of escape from this vengeful man and his monstrous hound that now regarded him balefully. 'A remote farm hard by Goonhilly Downs, owned by an uncle. His good wife nursed me to health, while a shipwright from Cadgwith fashioned the leg. I still heard news, though, even there. Such as the day on which you were apprehended.'

'The *Falcon* survivors tracked me down,' Trevanion admitted. 'Cornered me in a barn behind Talland church. They'd have beaten me to a bloody pulp had not the Reverend Dodge and Squire Polglaze, the magistrate, heard the clamour and intervened. They sent for the Militia and you now know the remainder of the tale. The commuting of my death sentence came only in the nick of time for me, but yours, old friend, comes this night. And it shall not be commuted.'

Kneebone now knew in what form his fate would come, and that Trevanion had been moving as he spoke, cleverly positioning Kneebone to a spot from where he could not escape, his back to the cliff and the terrible drop beyond. Trevanion pointed a long finger at the hapless Kneebone and rapped out his final command.

'Bosun…… kill!'

By God, but the thing was bigger than a Shetland pony, and lean with muscle and sinew. Kneebone saw it crouch for the spring, growling deep in its throat, manic deathlight in its eyes, lips curling back from sharp yellow teeth of fearsome length and which froze Kneebone's blood at the sight of them. And then it sprang.

In hope born of sheer desperation, Kneebone used his good leg to hurl himself aside as the hound, snarling horribly, leapt at him. He felt a momentary impact on his wooden leg, then heard the snarls turn to a frantic, forlorn yelping that diminished and diminished as the animal's body twisted helplessly through two hundred feet of void. The pitiful cries ceased abruptly and Kneebone's ears caught the dreadful sound of impact, far below. With his heart racing, Kneebone pulled himself up onto his knee.

'*Bosun!*' came the cry from the distraught Trevanion. 'You bastard, Kneebone, to do for my hound!' And then the man was on him, hauling him up and raising a dagger high above Kneebone's head. Desperately, he grasped the bony wrist, striving to prevent the dagger's descent. Locked in the deadliest of combats, the two men turned and twisted on the edge of the cliff, but the bigger man's strength was beginning to tell, the point of the dagger coming ever closer to Kneebone's face and throat, despite all of his own best efforts. In sheer hope and little more, Kneebone hooked his fingers deep into the man's wrist, wrenching his own wrist and Trevanion's inward until he heard a sickening crack of bone.

Trevanion's fight slackened with the sudden pain, giving Kneebone a second in which to twist and push away the point of the weapon that remained in Trevanion's grasp, and to drive it deep into the remaining eye. The scream that followed was terrible. The man's violent reaction to the searing pain threw Kneebone onto his back. He kicked out, the toe of his good leg catching the blinded Trevanion square in the groin and staggering him back until there was no turf left to stagger on. For a second, and shorn of his sight, Trevanion had no notion of what was happening. Then terrible realisation set in, and the man shrieked horribly until his bone-shattering impact on unyielding rock scant feet away from the lifeless carcass of his canine accomplice in serial murder.

Trembling with surges of adrenalin from the terror of his experience, Kneebone turned himself onto his front, using his hands to pull himself forward and peer over the brink. Far below, barely visible in the moonlight, the eyeless corpse of Piers Trevanion lay shattered on a shelf of rock, yards from the broken body of his monstrous hound. Within an hour, he knew, the rising spring tide would take them both, and most likely, neither one would be seen again.

Kneebone shuffled back from the edge, finding a handhold on the branches of a stunted tree to haul himself upright, panting for breath.

'Long are the years, Piers Trevanion, since you took my leg,' he said quietly, 'and I took your eye. Yet even that was insufficient for you. For twenty years, you sought my death, and have only bought your own. One good turn deserves another indeed, and I'll be the last man grieving. Lend my regards to Old Nick when you meet him.'

John and the Piskies

Many of our Cornish peasants work in the mines, or in mine-related industries for much of the year, but when Spring comes, and there's need for workers on the farms for planting and again in Autumn for harvesting. Many look to the farms for employment. Many, in fact, live in buildings on those farms the year round, and work their rent when needed. Both ways of making a meagre living are hard and rigorous, but such is the fate of those not born to property. It seems to be God's plan, and I decline to question it. 'The rich man in his castle, the poor man at his gate……' as we sing on Sunday.

My home is, of course, is near Wendron, and it is in that vicinity that I do my Church-wardenry and much of my personal business. It is also where I am most likely to encounter my 'friendly enemy' John Kneebone.

One Autumn, riding on my round of the dwellings of the Poor and Indigent – pursuant to my duties as Overseer – I came upon a group of farm labourers resting by a stream. I saw familiar faces – Daniel and his son Daniel John, Benny and a few others, and, in their midst, was Kneebone.

I knew very well that he hadn't been working with them. His lack of leg disqualified him, legitimately I must admit, from many occupations, and field labour was one of them. They were apparently satisfied to have him in their company – they knew him well – and probably were willing to share some of their refreshments with him in exchange for a tale. These were men who were not to be taken in by his lies. Nonetheless, a bit of entertainment was worth paying for. I stopped under a tree and led my horse to the stream for a drink. As I led him back to the path, sure enough, I heard Kneebone start:

Are you sure you want to know how I lost my leg? You won't believe me, I'm certain of that. It all started when I was working for ol' farmer Bawden up Trewennack. Back then I was as fit and as strong as the next man and everyone said I was one of his best day labourers. It was September, just as the leaves were beginning to fade from their lively summer green into the burnt russet of autumn, and so was coming close to harvest time.

Farmer Bawden was in desperate need of men to bring in his crops before the winter rains came and they started turning. Have you ever smelled the stench of a field full of cabbages rotting in the earth? I tell you it isn't pleasant and best avoided if possible. There were many of us at that point so no matter how hard the work was we managed to complete it in good time. After a hard day's work in the fields, me and the other workers would return to the farmhouse to be rewarded with a home cooked meal and a fresh cup of cider from the farmer's orchards. I can hear my stomach grumbling just thinking about it. It has been a long time since I ate so hearty a meal as I did back then.

Although I remember my time there fondly, it is obvious with hindsight that something was amiss at the farm. Workers who had been in the prime of health one moment would take ill suddenly and we would all watch them waste away from sickness, unable to keep food or drink down. Most would leave the farm to seek a doctor or take rest back at home with their families, but many were not so lucky. It was during the height of the harvest that farmer Bawden's workforce had dwindled to almost nothing. Just five men to bring in acres of food. No matter how good we were, it wasn't possible to do it all by ourselves. And as fast as we could hire more men, others would fall sick or leave, fearing for their lives.

It was dire. I worried for ol' Bawden's livelihood, his farm and his young wife and children who would not be able to sustain themselves if they could not bring the harvest in to sell. Bawden had taken me in when I had no place to go, gave me work and shelter and his family had shown me nothing but kindness. In return I worked harder for him than any man I knew. I even looked after his wife when he had to go away on business. As an honourable man, I owed it to him to find the cause of the sickness and save the farm.

That day I began my search. For hours I looked all over, checking the food stores, water sources and anything else that could possibly make people sick. By the end of the day, however, I was feeling more disheartened than ever as I had found nothing that might explain why the farmhands were dropping like flies. I decided to take a break and leant against one of the apple trees in the orchard. The warmth of the evening sun quickly pulled me downwards into the grip of exhausted sleep.

When I awoke, night had already fallen. Stars winked at me, squinting through the branches and apples above my head, and the large moon hung lazily in the cloudless sky. My body was stiff from sitting in such an awkward position in the cool night air, but as I began to push myself off the ground I heard voices nearby and quickly dropped back to my knees. One of the few benefits of having one leg is that now I only have one knee that aches! The voices were high and airy, like listening to the wind through a crack underneath a door and I couldn't quite make out what they were saying, but I heard them laughing about something. Although they sounded like merry folk, something told me that they wouldn't be so happy if they found out I was listening to them. I hid myself behind some nearby gorse bushes and scratched myself up something proper in the process. The voices stopped and for a moment I feared they had heard me but soon they were back to laughing and joking.

As I peered through the bushes, tiny figures holding flaming lanterns came into view. They were about the size of children, but looked just like you or I and wore the garb of hunters and highwaymen. I watched as they wandered the orchard together, taking the best apples from the ground and placing them into their pockets – which never seemed to be full, even when the largest of apples were placed inside. The fire of their lanterns danced in front of them as they foraged. Moths were drawn to it and frolicked in and out of the darkness. I felt the draw of their warmth and light too and more than once had to catch myself from revealing myself and walking towards the beckoning light. It was then that I realised who these little people were. There was no doubt they were piskies, mischievous sprites that led travellers into danger for the fun of it. I'd heard plenty of tales from droll-tellers in dark taverns, but I'd never seen them myself.

Once they had gathered enough apples, they began to leave the orchard. Not in the direction they had come back towards the moors, instead they were creeping towards the press house where Bawden made his delicious cider. Whatever mischief they were planning to make on the poor farmer and his family I had to know – so I followed a few paces behind them. Once they were inside, as quickly and as quietly as I could I clambered up the uneven stone wall of the barn and peered through the window into the dusty building.

The piskies were already hard at work making cider. They had dumped the apples into the heavy granite mill to grind up into pulp and to my surprise it was moving on its own without a pony in sight! I watched as they gathered the pulp into layers of hay and with a flick of a finger the giant wooden beam of the press lifted up and came down hard on it. Golden juice flowed out of the grooves in the beam press and into the awaiting barrels. The pisky-folk had accomplished in mere moments what would normally take days to do.

I was so dumbfounded by the sight that I almost slipped and fell from my perch and missed the most important part of the process. One of the piskies, who wore a red cap and was possibly the most beautiful creature I have seen before or since – including my long-suffering wife, dear of her – went from barrel to barrel and sprinkled shining powder that sparkled like fire into each one. The group then rolled their fresh barrels into the cellar along with the farmer's to ferment and mature. They then opened up some of the older barrels and took a triumphant sip to check the flavour.

Then, as quickly as they had started their work, each pisky shrunk down to nothing and vanished leaving no trace behind but their barrels.

It was almost morning, so when I climbed down to check their work I was met by farmer Bawden coming down the path on his way to feed the pigs.

'What are you doing hanging around the cider barn so early, John?' He said to me. Well I told him of course! I told him the whole story and what do you know? He didn't believe me. In fact, he went so far as to accuse me of being up all night drinking!

That was a hard day's work on no sleep and only a handful of other men to help out, but we got through it somehow. That night however Henry, one of the labourers, fell ill. He was vomiting and clutching his belly like the rest of them – and you know what? He'd just had a big mug of cider fresh from the barrel. Something had to be done. I excused my myself and headed back to the barn to lie in wait for the piskies to start work.

I hid behind the barrels and waited. I waited so long I was about to give up hope of them returning until I heard laughter and song from outside, echoing up from the orchard. Soon the barn door creaked open and there they were, the same little men as before with the one in the red cap leading them. He must have been in charge, perhaps the king, if piskies have those. They began walking towards the machines but I wasted no time and leapt from my hiding spot. I lunged towards them, but they were too fast and jumped out of the way whenever I got close. Once I thought I had one, but they changed their shape and shrunk down to the size of a mouse and scurried away laughing. My momentum carried me forward and I toppled over, sprawling onto the ground. Their laughter continued and they began to sing:

'John Kneebone, John Kneebone

You're much too slow to win this fight

You meddle with what you don't understand

And for your hubris we take your sight'

As soon as they chanted that last word, all went dark. I could still hear them giggling and taunting me as they carried on their work but could not find them. I heard the grinding of the granite mill, the flowing juice and the rolling of barrels across the cobblestone floor. Finally, I heard them open the older barrels and take a triumphant sip to check the flavour. I had failed.

The next morning, Bawden found me once more in the cider barn, but I only knew him from his voice. And you know what he said.

'What are you doing hanging around the cider barn so early, John?'

Well I told him of course. I told him the whole story. And showed him that I was now blind thanks to the magic of the piskies. Yet he still did not believe me. He told me I'd just had too much strong cider and that my sight loss was temporary. He was in a mind to kick me off his farm, but he needed what man power he could muster, so he put me to work. Luckily for me, he was right to a degree and the pisky magic wore off later that day. But It was clear I needed to rethink my plan. Another of the farmhands fell ill that night because of my failure so I had to try again. Fighting the pisky-folk would not work, but maybe I could talk to them.

I hid, just as I had done the night before but when the piskies came, this time I did not leap out at them. I stood slowly and raised my hands above my head to show I meant no harm. They instantly stopped their jovial singing and became defensive.

'I just want to talk,' I told them. They watched but made no reply. 'People are falling ill after drinking the cider-'

'It is not for you.' Said their leader in the red cap.

'It gets mixed up with our cider,' I said. 'Why not just have some of ours? We have plenty to share. I can attest that it's good stuff!'

'It is not for us.' Said the pisky in the red cap.

'But-' I began but they cut me off as they started singing again.

'John Kneebone, John Kneebone
You've made another terrible choice
Children should be seen, not heard
So for your arrogance we take your voice'

I tried to speak, but no sound came out. I screamed into the silence and was met with more laughter from the piskies as they carried on with their work. So I watched. I made a note of every barrel they filled with pisky cider and an idea came to my head. When they finished, they opened up the older barrels and took a triumphant sip to check the flavour, then vanished as before. When they were gone, I began pouring farmer Bawden's cider into the piskies' barrels, mixing it together as best I could so that they would not be able to tell it had been tampered with. If pisky cider made humans sick, perhaps human-made cider would be poisonous to piskies. It was long work as the barrels were too heavy to lift, so I had to scoop out the cider with mugs and as the first rays of morning light broke through the window, I was still mixing. It was in such a position that farmer Bawden found me.

'What are you doing hanging around the cider barn so early, John?' He said. I opened my mouth to try to tell him of course, I wanted to tell him the whole story, but I could not speak.

'Your throat is so dry from drinking cider all night!' He said, 'Go and drink some water at once. Then get to work before I have you carted off!'

'I nodded and did as I was told, I couldn't argue even if I wanted to, and I knew that I only needed one more night to sort out the problem and save the farm. I worked hard in that knowledge and with no voice to distract anyone with idle chitchat we just barely managed to complete the days work with only three men. By that evening, my voice had returned but I had no time to use it in the usual merry-making. I had more work to do. This time, I took my place at the window just like I did the first night and waited for the piskies to arrive.

'When they arrived they didn't start work straight away, they searched the barn looking for me.

'Must have learned his lesson finally,' I heard one of them say when they could not find me anywhere. Another struck up a working song as they started the process. I watched as they pulped the apples. I watched as they pressed the pulp. I watched as they poured the juice into barrels. I watched as the pisky in the red cap sprinkled fire into the cider. Then came the moment I had been waiting for. All the piskies gathered around the older barrels and began opening them. They took out cups and dipped them into the cider, filling them to the brim and lifting them to their mouths. I held my breath as in turn, they took a sip, swallowing the mixture. For a few moments, nothing happened and I worried that my plan had not worked.

'Suddenly, one of the piskies bent double and began to be sick. The others soon felt the effects too and whatever magic they used to change shape began to malfunction. Some rocketed upwards, others shrank. Some grew great bushy beards, others turned into simple forest creatures, but all were sick and writhing on the rough barn floor. I was so happy the plan had worked that I let out a cheer in my excitement. The pisky in the red cap, now a horrid cross between man and fox, looked up and saw me and let out a terrible yell.

'John Kneebone, John Kneebone

You ignored our warnings yet again

Your meddling has left us legless

So for your deeds we do you the same'

And with the final word of his curse, he disappeared to nothing, along with the rest of his group, leaving behind toppled barrels and cider spilt throughout the barn. Just as I thought I had won I started to feel a tingle in the toes of my left foot. It began to spread across the bridge and around my ankle and before I knew what was happening I saw my boot fall away to the ground below me. Where my flesh should have been was nothing but air. The tingle continued to creep up my leg, devouring my calf and thigh, and I could only look on in horror as the entirety of my left leg disappeared completely, the same way the piskies had done. My now empty trouser leg flapped limply in the breeze and I lost my hold on the windowsill and hit the earth with a thud.

Farmer Bawden found me lying in the bushes the next morning, with one less leg than he remembered me having, and an almighty mess in his press house. He was furious. He didn't even ask me what I was doing hanging around the cider barn so early, and he certainly did not believe my story. But there was no blood and, although they searched, they never did find my leg. Unlike my sight and speech, it didn't come back later that day. I was allowed to stay long enough to regain my strength, but as I could no longer work I was given a crutch and sent off to wander Cornwall alone.

So there you have it, that's the story of how I lost my leg. No one on Bawden's farm ever got sick again after that night and his farm became one of the most successful in the parish. Coincidentally it's also the story of how I single-handedly chased the pisky cider production out of Cornwall and into Devon. You see, up country they're dealing with the Devon Colic, the symptoms of which are suprisingly similar to the illness that took Bawden's men, but there isn't any of it in Cornwall. The piskies wouldn't dare risk crossing me again. So if you enjoy your cider, you've got me to thank for it. Bawden never did!

'Good Morning to 'ee, Squire Wearne, and to these two fine gent'men withee'

I winced inwardly at this, knowing the voice which seemed to creep up on one from behind, as was the habit of its owner. I had heard that Kneebone was out of gaol but had hoped that he might not be in Helston so soon.

'Good morning, John.' I replied. 'I hope that you are keeping yourself well and occupied.'

'Oh, middlin' well, considerin', sir. The old troubles plague me, and the Missis is poorly, but I keep a fair face to the sun nonetheless. Don't you find that's the way to be, sirs?'

I was more than a little alarmed that he chose to address himself to my companions, they being strangers in Cornwall, newly arrived from America with a cargo of cotton. I had had no cause to warn them about Kneebone, of course, he not being on my mind at all. Poor fellows, they replied before I could give them so much as a cautionary shake of the head.

'Why, I suppose so, sir. It's best to maintain a positive attitude.' One of them – a trader from Boston – replied politely.

'Well – bless me!' Exclaimed Kneebone. 'Do I mark the accents of the Colonies to the West? Good it is for my soul to hear again the honest speech of Amerikee as I heard it on those shores long ago!'

'Now John,' I cautioned, 'I was not aware that you had been across the sea. My impression was that your whole life had been compassed within Kerrier, save for sojourns in Bodmin.' I knew this to be fact, but wanted to keep the conversation gentle.

'Well it just shows that even a fine gent and a Churchwarden at that may not know everything that there is to know under the liberty-loving sun, now don't it?' Kneebone muttered with the hint of a snarl out of the corner of his mouth in my direction. 'These gentlemen (and I didn't catch their names) seem to be open-minded sorts and not prejudiced against a man just because he's temporarily down on 'is luck. They would shake a poor man's hand, now wouldn't they? And speak their names like free and honest men, sez I.'

At this, of course, my companions graciously, and with a touch of humour, shook Kneebone's hand pronounced their names (we'll call them Smith and Jones) and their homes and stations quite graciously.

'And I be John Kneebone, of Wendron, Sithney and Gweek, temporarily without occupation, at your service, I'm sure, gentlemen.' Kneebone said with a nod of the head.

'I'm pleased to make your acquaintance, Mr. Kneebone' said Smith politely.

'MISTER, is it? Thankee kindly sir. There's some here,' He said with the slightest of glances at me, 'who could learn a manner or two from our American friends, it seems.'

'Kneebone?' Asked Jones. 'Not a name I've run across before. Is it a common name here?'

'Common? Not common in the one sense at all, sir, but in another common enough to be found in nearly every parish in Cornwall. We're a populatin' bunch, we Kneebones. In fact, there're Kneebones in Amerikee – my cousin Bob emigrated last year, an' his brother Tom before him.

'And…' Here Kneebone's voice smoothed itself a bit as a light came into his eye. A light I knew too well. I inwardly groaned and prepared myself for the inevitable.

'And I can vouch from my own knowledge of one kneebone that rests forever in Amerikee, if you catch my meaning.'

It took a moment for the light to dawn on my companions, but with a slight motion of his head, Kneebone directed their gaze to his lower half.

'Ah! So you lost your leg in America? Well, well, what an unfortunate circumstance. How did it happen?'

'Well, we're for it now!' I said to myself. Fortunately, there was a bench in front of the office from which we had just emerged, and I sat to rest myself during what I knew to be coming.

'Y'see, sir – it was like this. As a lad, I went to sea. There had been a bit of a misunderstandin' between myself and a local shopkeeper. He said I had made off wi' some needles and a few yards of linen, when I had told 'im very distinkly that my mother would be by d'reckly to pay. Well – Mother never got the chance to defend me – I was whisked off to Magistrate and given the choice of a year in gaol or a year at sea with the Merchant Navy.

"Well," I sez – "Me for the open sea!" and next I knew I was in Plymouth climbing a gangplank.

'The ship's Mate took me by the ear – this 'ere ear, mind you sir – and shoved me down into the kitchens. "'Ere's yer new Tweenie, Jack" he said to the cook, and that was my name from there on – as long as I was on that there ship.

'I 'ardly saw the light of the sun for the next few weeks, no I didn't, sir. That hard old cookie kept me at peelin', cleanin', carryin' and servin' from dawn to dark, and no miner ever got paler from depreevation of light than I did, and that's a fact. I hardly knew whether we was asea or in port most o' the time. One thing, though. I never got ill of it. No seasick for Tweeny. Now the cook, he 'uz plagued with it and never passed a day on board without sickin' up. So you see how I found a deal of 'is work fallin' on my shoulders, to boot.'

'A hard life, the life of a Seaman, to be sure!' said Smith.

'Seaman you say! Not but wot I was considderd one o' they. Bilge rat, they called me! Lubber as well even when they was as green as limes from a followin' wind! No, no Seaman was I by their lights.

'Well, to get along….'

'At last!' I thought to myself.'

'Now one day in the port of Lisbon, the day came when His Worship the Capting called me into his quarters. I threw off my apron and knocked at his door, my heart in my mouth. "Here, boy," 'e said,

"Take this to the Captain of the Marie, just to our port, there." An' he handed me a cloth bag. I pulled the forlock and sed "Aye, Sir" and skeedaddled, as I could tell by the feel that it was a bag of coins!

'I rolled down that gangway fast as I could and found the Marie straightaway. It were flyin' French colors, but I thought nothing of that. I'd be on and off before they could try any French tricks on me, I thought. I said to the first Frenchie I seed "Kap-ee-tain?" That bein' the way they say Capting, as you well know, sir.'

'Close enough.' Said Jones.

'He p'inted at a man with a feather in his hat, leaning on the rail. An' this Kap-ee-tain spoke to me in English! I wuz glad to hear it but not glad to hear wot he said. I'd been traded to the Frenchies! I never found out for what, and the bag wuz part of the value – it an' me – that was my old Capting's side of the bargain.

'Me on a French ship! Speakin' no French! Among strangers and foreigners! Sirs, I never spent a more mizzerble time in my life than I did as a lad on that French tub. I'd got used to the English sailors' smells, But never 'customed myself to those Frenchers. And once I learned some of their talk, I found that they were the most scurvy, foul-spoken and immoral lot of louts to be found on the sea or land.

'My job was as a sort of Cabin-Boy. No more kitchen, thank God (beggin' yer pardon, Squire Wearne.) I had the run of the ship and found plenty of time to rest and recuperate in that lax French crew. Mind you, some of they Frenchies had odd ideas about what a cabin-boy's duties was, and I'll say no more but that by this time I had got my growth and was able to fend off the nasty bug...... rather – sailors, if you'll grant me yer pardon. Y'see – but for the way I'm now crippled up, all bent and broke under my cruel maiming and the cares and woes of a poor man's life I'd stand as tall as you fine trees of gentlemen, and a bit taller, too, at that.

'So after a few weeks on that French scow, I noticed that we were maintainin' a westerly headin' and asked as best I could where we was bound.'

"Ah-mare-eek" was the answer. Which as you learned gents know, is "America" in their oily tongue. So there I was, bound for America on a foreign ship, not knowing when or if I'd see the rocks of Cornwall again, and headed for a fate I knowed not what.

'Well, sirs, it was a rough cruise to be sure. We was three weeks in the going, and all of it bouncing like a cork. Three days out of five it were too rough to cook, so we – those what could still eat, of course – lived on hardtack and water. And rum, though the officers – mostly they was among the sick – never knowed it.

'We put in at the Azores, and it came to my mind to jump ship, but one look at those flea-bitten, mizzerbul pin-pricks of islands made even our stinking ship look like the Gardings of Babylonn, if you take my meaning, sirs. It seemed to me better to bide my time 'tween decks and try my luck in Amerikee.

'As we crossed, I were able to piece together what we wuz about. I'm none to meedle in the affairs of Kings and such deer, but it seemed as if France was at odds with Spain just then, and much had to do with propt'y in the New World. Particularly as regarded a place with the odd name of Penn-so-kola. Or as near as I could make out. We was to head there and try to get that place away from the Spanish.

'I looked it over and "Well," sed I, "we ain't no warship!" One nine-pounder and a couple kegs of powder wuddn't take no town bigger'n Polperro from any Spaniards, I reckoned. But we was to be a sort of "tender" I gathered, shipping supplies from one Man-O-War to another and to and from shore. Well now, you Gent'men know full well that you can get just as dead on a tender as on the "Royal Sovereign!" Let's just say that I weren't comfitted at not being a gunboat.

'We didn't go straight to Pensacoler. We first made land (blessed were the day that that crossing ended, and, ef I may say so, Sirs, dubble-blessed to be on the shores of Amerikee!) at B'luxi. It seemed that on board our ship were a High Vazeer of the French court, the "Soor de Serinee," and he were just all-fired to go find his brother – who seemed to command the French forces thereabout. La Moyne were his name. Well we kicked our heels against the hull at B'luxi for a week, with no shore leave, mind you, until our Capting came back aboard and rattled off a battery of French words, which included 'Pensacole.' You didn't have to be a lingist to guess where we was bound for next. Sure enough, one of my mates who had a bit of English cursed and let me know that we were for the thick of it, and God bless our widows.

The Spaniards had Pensakolee and the French wanted it. I knew it weren't no affair of mine, being a loyal Briton who knowed his dooty, but there I was. I allowed as it was my part to stay alive through it all and somehow get back to my ship or, in any event, a British ship or garrison, of which I had heard there was some in Boston or some such, which I 'sumed would be a short walk North'ard.

'It would break your kind hearts, sirs, to hear much of what went on when we got to Pensakolee. French though they wuz, it took my heart to see those brave seamen get blown to bits. Still, we won out in the end. Well, for a while. The French Flag flew over Pensacolly when the smoke cleared. Spanish prisoners were offered a choice – jine the French or take ship to Cuba. Some stayed, some went, and the ones who stayed must 'ave cursed their luck afore many more months passed.

'It were a hot, wet summer in French Pensakooley that year (and every year, I've come to understand.) We lived it up to the extent possible, Sirs. If yer not too much of churchmen, I'd tell tales of our hijinks and lowjinks that'ud make a Saint chuckle. But a Saint ain't no match for Churchwarden Wearne, 'ere, so I'll leave be. Anyway – all of that came to a sad end, sadder still for me, as you'll see, when the Spanish returned.

39

'One morning the shore-watch called out from his tower – nar – screamed, more like – and we all looked to sea. The horizon was jagged with ships. One Frenchie with a glass turned white as he peeped and gasped out: "Espanole!" We all lit out fer our dooty stations to do wut we could to save ourselves. I dashed back (and it was my last dash, Sirs. My last in this life) to my ship and up the gangway. The Capting and the Mate were roaring orders I couldn't understand, and the crew were scrambling like monkeys so I, not wantin' to impede progress, took it on myself to guard the fo'c'sle.

'That, sirs, was the worst choice I ever made in my life. I felt the ship cast off and try to catch some wind, though the tide couldn't help us. What our heading was, I couldn't tell from behind my barr…. from my guard post, but we lagged along as best as could be. What the Capting thought he was about, I'm shure I couldn't say, that day or this.

'Soon enough I heard shots and smelled powder. I could tell that our lone nine-pounder was being fired, although we were but a muss-keeter to those great Spanish galleons. One of um must have wanted us swatted though, it seems, as soon our ship shuddered with the force of a mighty blow. I heard some French screams and more French curses after that, as shake after shake told the story of our further demolition.

'My position in the fo'c'sle seemed secure enough that I felt I could maintain my vigilance even if the Capting ordered "Abandon ship." I thought that maybe I could weather that shelling until, with one almighty blow, an unseen hand smashed a ball into us 'midships, making our poor little tub leap like a wounded deer, and sent the mainmast directly through the fo'c'sle. And, kind sirs – tho it'll break yer hearts, I must say it – through my poor left leg.

'The sharp edge of an iron ring, fresh-sheared and red-hot from the cannon ball, sliced through my poor limb like a knife through butter just here, below the hip. I was just aware enough to feel myself thrown into the air, along with a large piece of decking. I knew no more until some Spanish sailors fished me and my raft up to the shoreline and splashed some rum down my throat. I looked down and saw my poor wrecked leg. The slick cut ampootated it as clean as a surgeon, and the heat from the iron ring cotterized it. That's what saved me from bleedin' to death.

'But there I was, maimed, helpless, alone and a prizzner. And sirs, you'll scarcely credit it, but as I live and die an honest man, that day was my thirteenth birthday!'

I moaned inwardly at the obviousness of this pathetic appeal, and hoped that my companions would not be too much taken in. But I soon learned, to my dismay, that Kneebone was not yet finished.

'So there I wuz, Sirs. My hopes crushed with my leg and no place to go. Well – I'll say this fer them Spanyards. They were kinder to a stranger than the French. They took me along to their field-hospital on shore and a surgeon did wot 'ee could to patch up my poor stump. For a couple of weeks after, though, I was down with the fever and I guess they didn' 'spec me to live through it. Little do they know the Cornish constitution, sirs. I shook and shivered enough to break three cots in them weeks, but at the end I came up strong and well, if a bit peakied.

'After I was able to talk, they realized that I weren't no Spanyer' nor Frenchie neither. Another patient a few cots down recognized my talk as English (uv a sort, Sirs. My great poverty had seeped into my tongue and I couldn't speak as ellygant as now, y'see.) Well, come time fer me to get up, they gimme a crutch (of wich I've worn out dozens in my weary travels and travailes, gent'men) and wisht me "Bayna Sairtay" which is the best they can do at 'Good Luck.' As they din't hold much with my being any sort o' spy or such all, bein'a cripple, they let me go my way.

'But what way, sirs? Well I could tell you all the trouble I had, a fresh cripple, on the roads of Amerikee, but suffuse it to say that I soon found meself on my way to a place called "New Orleens." I hear it's a great city now, but then – hardly a hunred 'ouses if they c'd be called such like. But there was a port of sorts there. I made my way by clumpin' along on my crutch and snagging rides on the odd cart, often sharing the ride wi' pigs or worse.

'I finally arrived in New Orleens, and took up a spot by the water to beg (aye, it's been my sorry fortune to have to beg for a livin, sirs, though you'd never credit it now.) Weeks went by before I heard the accents of home on some sailor-men fresh from sea. I fell on them like long-lost brothers and they took pity. When I 'eard that their cook had got drunk and been washed overboard a week gone by, I said "Mates, I'm yer man!"

'I said "An honester, soberer and cannyer sea-cook you've never met than old Kneebone!" I sed, sed I. Well – they took me to their Capting an' he reckon'd I'd be no likelier to pizen them than anyone else they cud find in that hole, so I 'ad a new berth!

'And it weren't more than three months later I set foot, (Jus' the one, mind) on British soil again, and swore I'd never lay a hand on what wasn't mine ever agin' in my life – seein' as how it had cost a year of that life and half my total of legs! And – kiss the book, sirs – I've kept straight since.'

I restrained myself at this point, seeing as how my companions had rather enjoyed Kneebone's tale, and when we parted with John with many a "Har-Har" and clasp of good fellowship, Smith (or maybe it was Jones) tucked a small bag, containing coin, I suspect, into Kneebone's sleeve.

'Ar – sir – ya don't know how much of a kindness you've done me an' my Missus. I'll admit to needin' the help of honest men at this terrible time. Thankee and God bless 'ee. And may He keep 'ee well as you return to that wonderful land where a part of me will always abide!'

May You Never Thirst

The tales I'm assembling here have come to me in unexpected ways, some of them at least. I was chatting about the stories over coffee recently, in a coffeehouse in Liskeard, with a friend, when an elderly Nonconformist clergyman, whom I thought had been dozing at a nearby table suddenly raised his hatbrim and fixed an eye on us. He chimed in without prelude as follows:

'Some years ago I was sitting on a bridge over the River Lynher at Stara Bridge on my way to Linkinhorne church where I knew the Kneebones had been the vicars in days long ago, when a man came by. Nothing strange in that you may think, except he had the most beautifully carved wooden leg and a crutch to match. It was so fine that I had to comment on it.'

"Well" said the man, "There is a story about how I came by these if you have a few minutes." And with that he began his tale:

"'I'll have you know that I am a God-fearing man. So much so that I will visit any chapel or church that I happen to be passing to praise the Lord and perhaps be welcomed with a bowl of soup or some bread and cheese. I'm happy to talk to ministers and priests of all faiths, but this time … well, let me start at the beginning…

"After many miles of wandering the lanes of South East Cornwall I knew I had to find somewhere to lay my weary body for the night and, if the locals were able, to find someone to provide me with a bite to eat and perhaps even a small jug of ale. It was getting late in the day and the sun was just starting on her downward path towards her rest and I knew that, as soon as she had gone, I would be enveloped in darkness, it would prove more difficult to persuade someone to open their door to me. Down yet more narrow lanes I trudged but there was nothing and nowhere likely to rest my head when, something inside me said 'take the next lane'.

"A few more steps brought me to the entrance of a very narrow lane and as I looked in the distance I could see a sharp tor, outcrops on the horizon and the unmistakeable outline of engine houses. I knew I still had at least another day's walk before I reached them so made up my mind to find a sheltered hedgerow to nestle down in for the night. The lane seemed to be going slightly down hill and I thought it might lead down to the river where I could have a wash and fill up my bottle with water for my long trek the next morning, so I began to follow it. Much to my surprise, as I rounded the bend, there stood an isolated farmhouse, larger than most, slate hung and capped with the same. Surely a house of some importance. To the side there was a range of stables so I hoped they might afford me shelter for the night.

"Tapping gently on the kitchen door, I waited tentatively to see what the reaction would be to a weary traveller asking for food and shelter. Gently the door opened and there in the half shadows stood a round, portly woman, rubbing her hands on her apron. The warmth of the kitchen and all the goodly smells launched themselves at me until I was enveloped in them and my heart lifted.

"In front of the fire, with a stomach full of good stew and a jug of small beer in my hand, my feet warming and knowing I had a bed for the night, the old woman began to relate the task she had to complete if anyone came to the door asking for food and shelter. Her husband, now back from a long day in the fields, settled with us and, with shutters closed and logs piled up both sides of the fire, she began to tell the story.

"'Many, many years ago', she began, 'in a time before any of us can remember but in a time we are reminded of every day when we look to the moors, an old druid priest came walking down the same lane as you today. He too was looking, as you were, for food and lodging, somewhere to lay his tired and feeble bones. Seeing Rillaton Manor he knocked on the door, fully expecting to be welcomed, after all he was a priest. Such was his surprise when the door was thrown open and the Lord of the Manor stood there, tankard in hand and roaring at him to be off and never to walk his lands or he would set his dogs on him. The priest begged for the shelter of the stables as it was winter and the winds were bitterly cold and the sky promised snow. This only made the Lord of the Manor even more angry.

"'Just some water', the priest begged.

"'Never' came the angry reply. The old priest walked away with all the dignity he could muster. He stopped at the gate, looked back saying, 'Bless you, may you never thirst.' The door was slammed and the priest walked down the lane looking for a hedgerow to shelter him from the coming weather.

"Next morning, huddled under wet leaves and a blanket of snow, the frozen body of the old priest was found by one of the farm workers on his way to tend his cattle. Realising this was a man of some importance, a priest, the farmworker ran to fetch his friends and family to take the priest to his final resting place. Gently and reverently they laid him out in a shallow grave on the top of the moors nearby and with him they laid his possessions, a gold cup, a sword and a knife. Over his body they heaped the granite stones and boulders to keep him safe from scavenging animals.

"When the Lord of the Manor heard what had happened he felt no remorse at all and laughed at the foolishness of the priest. 'Serves him right', he laughed, 'coming here expecting me to shelter him and give him food and drink just because he was a priest!'

"Days passed and the winter began to take its toll. Food was scarce and the wild animals came down from the moors to feed from what they could find around any of the isolated houses. One night, as he was stabling his horse, the Lord of the Manor heard a terrible growling in the yard and saw the eyes of a wild black dog, foam dripping from its mouth. Before he could draw his sword, the dog jumped at him and bit him. He ran inside the manor house, fearing what was to come.

In the days that followed he began to feel most unwell, and had a ravaging thirst that could not be slaked, for, every time he put a cup of water to his lips, he shrieked in fear and threw it to the other side of the room. The old priests' words came back to him, 'May you never thirst'. Perhaps, he thought, if I had given him water this would not be happening to me. 'Oh God help me', he cried over and over again as he knew his end was fast approaching. 'This one last thing I command', he called to his family and servants. 'If anyone comes here asking for shelter and food and drink it must be given to them for now and for eternity.' Rabies racked his body and he died a fearful death crying out for water but unable to quench his thirst.'

"There was silence as the woman ended her story. I looked into my empty tankard and watched the shadows in the dying embers of the fire. 'So', I said, 'you still have to provide a dole of bread and ale and shelter to anyone who asks'.

"The kindly face of the woman looked up, 'yes', she said, 'sleep well'.

"The following morning, with a bottle full of small beer and a bag at my side full of food, I began on my way. Down the lane I walked, heading towards the moorland mining settlement where I knew the old priest's bones must still lie. The sound of babbling water caught my ear and there, a few yards around the corner, was the River Lynher. I followed the bank along until I met with another lane and saw, to my delight, the old packhorse Stara Bridge and sitting on the parapet, wearing the dark robes of a priest was an old man. I stopped to pass the time of day and he asked of me if I had been given good hospitality. 'The best', I said, 'and look at this bag of food I have to last me the next couple of days'. The old man examined the contents of my bag, sniffing gently at the still warm bread and home-made cheese.

"'Would you spare a little for me, he asked?' I opened my bag and spread a veritable feast before us and opened the bottle to share my small beer.

"Perhaps a half hour had passed when I said I had to be on my way as I had a long walk before me for I was heading up the moors to the village of Minions where I was sure to find work and a place to lay my head. The old man helped pack all the remains back in my bag and we took our goodbyes. A few steps and I heard him call out, 'May you never thirst', I turned to salute him but all I could see were a few crumbs where we had shared our meal.

"May you never thirst. The words echoed through me as a cold chill swept over my body. May you never thirst! Who was this man? What was this priest?

"I found my footsteps quickening and I broke into run. The cold chill stayed in my bones and I could still hear his words. No more stops for me, I decided, I would have to press on and make Minions before nightfall. There was no way I wanted to be caught in the dark with no shelter and the possibility of meeting up with him again … or perhaps the noises I heard in the fields and copses was a black dog, after all, I had heard stories that there were 3 black dogs roaming near here. Every picture raced through my mind as I hurried onwards and upwards.

 "Night was falling and I knew in my heart that I should stop and find shelter for the mining around Minions was well known for its treacherous landscape. I should never risk crossing this part of the moor in the dark for fear of …

"And then it happened. The thing I had warned myself of and the very reason I knew I should have stopped. But I was too spooked by my meeting with the old priest, and all the folklore and tales had woven themselves into my brain and crept through my body 'till I had forced myself to go on when I should have stopped.

"The pain seared through me. My screams rent the air and darkness fell around me. When I came to I knew what had happened at once. This part of the moor is, literally, speckled with old mining adits and spoil heaps. In the darkness of the night you cannot tell where you are putting your feet. As I lay there thoughts of what might happen raced through my mind. What should I do first? Would anyone hear me if I called out? The pain in my leg was dulling so I decide to try and feel my way in the darkness to see if there was an easy slope I could pull myself up. My screams rent the air as I realised exactly what I had done. My leg was bent under me and smashed. Fragments of bone stuck through my skin and I knew I would not be able to climb out. My only hope was to call and hope a passing miner or bal maiden would hear my cries. I knew they walked from miles around every day to get to the mines around here, after all, this was the largest mining complex in Cornwall and covered the whole of this part of the moors. Men would burrow in the granite to find tin, copper and silver, risking their lives daily to pull the precious ore from the land. They would have a doctor here, of that I was sure, but first I had to get out!

"All night I lay there listening to the muffled sounds above. What was that? A fox, a horse, a badger or a man? The sweat poured down and my shirt was sticking to me. My mouth was dry and the pain was sickening. All my adventures began to pass before me and I found myself thinking and remembering some of the people I had known, the fun times I had and with a heavy heart I began to realise that I might not actually ever be found and I might end my days lying in this adit. Minutes and hours crept by. Every time I heard a sound I called out for help but no help came. I prayed and prayed and readied myself to meet my maker.

"Just as the first rays of the dawn crept down the adit I heard it. Or did I? I called out but there was no answer. Another fox? another badger? Surely this was a different sound? There it was again. Laughter, I was sure. One last time I pulled myself up and cried out and screamed as if my life depended on it… well it did actually. But I heard nothing. I screamed again and heard a voice, the voice of a young girl frantically saying, 'I didn't imagine it, tell me it isn't a ghost.' I called again, 'Help me, help me, I have fallen in the adit. Help me'. When the voice of a man called 'Who's there?' I knew my prayers had been answered.

"The sun was well up as I was carried, on a door taken from an out building, up the moors to the mine. The pain was so bad that I kept falling in and out of consciousness but, deep down, I knew I was going to be well looked after and there would be a doctor there to help me. My mangled leg would be straightened out and, although it would take some weeks, I would be able to carry on my journey.

"I was laid on one of the crushing tables when we got there and the miners and Bal maidens crowded round. I fully expected one of the faces looking down at me to be the mine doctor but then it dawned on me. This was the mine where there had been unrest recently, where the miners were calling for the mine owners to employ a doctor. There was no doctor. A kindly face of an old woman looked down at me as she explained what she would do. She laid a poultice on my mangled leg and gave me a syrup to drink to help dull the pain. A doctor had been sent for from Liskeard, the local town, but it would take at least 5 or 6 hours to get there, find him and get him back out to the mine. This was why the miners wanted a doctor on site.

"As evening fell and the sun's rays dipped behind the Cheesewring, we heard it, wheels on the gravel and the clip clop of horses' hooves. The doctor had been found and he was here to set my leg. I heard them talking in muffled voices and saw the shaking of their heads. The doctor looked down at me and smiled as he pulled the bones in my leg straight and I knew no more.

"When I came to he had gone back to Liskeard and I was left in the kindly care of the old woman. 'There was no other way', she said as I looked at where my leg had once been. I sobbed and sobbed as wave after wave of self-pity flowed through me. If only I had not been so stupid to have been spooked by the old priest on the bridge. If only I hadn't listened to the old woman in the remains of Rillaton Manor. How stupid had I been!

"Days passed and I was tended with great care. The young maid that had heard my cries came to see me on her way back from the mine every day. Her father, the man who had pulled me from the adit, came when he could and piece by piece I was able to get the full story. It was miraculous they had found me. They walked the moors from their home in Henwood every day, him and his sons to mine the precious ores and she and her sisters to crush the stones and extract the tin. It was a dangerous place to work and accidents were common place. Death was a hazard you lived with. The Mine Owners took the money and gave back a pittance. 'So', I asked, one day as I sat with my back against the granite walls of Houseman's Shaft engine house, 'How can I repay you? I only have one leg so I can't work but there must be something I can do'.

"After what seemed like hours but was only a minute or two, the answer came. 'You are a man of words, we are men of hard rock mining and don't have the words. Help us to persuade the Mine Owners to have a doctor on site. If there had been one when we brought you in your leg may have been saved. We are treated poorly by them, our pay is given at the end of the month regardless of how many days there are. Help us to get it changed. We want to be paid every 4 weeks, not every month, we want to be treated well. We want to be treated, and respected, as humans, not like animals.'

"I looked up into the pleading eyes of the man who had saved my life.

"'Yes' was the only word I could say. I knew I was committing to something that was almost an impossibility but it was the least I could do.

"It was some months later that I walked away from Minions. My carved wooden leg supporting me and with a matching crutch, both made by the mine carpenter. The sun was coming up and it would be a warm day ahead. I had made so many friends here and it would be a difficult parting that I had decided to go before they came to grass or went down. I heard my name being called but walked on. I heard it again, this time with a sense of urgency. I looked back and there stood my friends. It was the Monday morning after pay day and in the past the mine would have stood empty. Mazed Monday they called it. The day when the drink taken over the weekend had been so bad as to split every head with pain. But not any more.

"'Where do you think you are going without saying your farewells?' The gnarled hands of the miners shook mine in grateful thanks, the bal maidens hugged me. But one hand was different and will stay with me all my days. It was the smooth hand of a surgeon doctor. 'Come on' he said, 'I'm going down to Liskeard today to pick up more medical supplies. I can give you a ride in my pony and trap'.

"Now you can read in your history books about the Great Strike at Minions Mine, the longest strike in mining history. You can read about how the Miners had to give up Mazed Monday and in return were given their pay every 4 weeks instead of every month and you can read about how the mine got a resident doctor and how many lives were saved because of it. But I can tell you the real story behind it and how, if it hadn't been for me losing my leg, they wouldn't have one to this day. But that's another story for another day…'"

Author's Note:

On Minions Moor lies the tomb of a druid priest and in it was found a gold cup, now in the British Museum, and a sword and a knife, now both lost. It is called the Rillaton Burrow and the Rillaton Gold Cup after the name of the Manorial lands where it was found. The Manor of Rillaton is long gone but the Dower House still stands and in the deeds to it is the clause that twice a year a dole of bread and ale must be given to the workers on the farm. So, twice a year, at harvest and at Wassail I give the dole to the local farmers and any friends who happen to drop by and, as part of it always bid them, may you never thirst. I own it. I'm taking no chances.

The mine at Minions did see the longest strike in Cornwall's mining history to this day. With no doctor on site it took over 6 hours to get to Liskeard, find a doctor, and get back, causing the deaths of so many miners and bal maidens. Having a doctor on site meant accidents that would have been major became minor and the men and women were able to continue to work and productivity was up. Some people will tell you that the strike failed because they had to give up Mazed Monday in return for a resident doctor and being paid every 4 weeks, which meant an extra pay packet a year. Any experienced union negotiator will tell you it was a win!

Pibrek

Isabella Bonython Smythe (Isabella B-S or IBS for short) had an imposing presence. She was a handsome, rather than elegant, figure and the considerable strain that she was clearly putting on some complex corsetry witnessed a life with little experience of that led by the less fortunate classes. She was wife of one Sir Charles Bonython Smythe, Magistrate of Helston. She was also impossible to say no to. This was why I found myself on a coach escorting the redoubtable John Kneebone to the Assizes currently and conveniently held in Bodmin Jail. I had business to attend to in the town and she was visiting her sister at St Bennets Abbey in nearby Lanivet. Having learned of her husband's decision to send Kneebone to

Bodmin she had decided that we would do the escorting rather than transport this 'poor damaged hero' manacled in the back of a cart.

Isabella B.S. also explained to me quietly in private that she had 'sent word to young Judge Jeffries' asking him to listen sympathetically to Kneebone's explanations, remember that he was a war hero and do the right thing by him. I was also aware that Isabella B.S.'s intelligence gathering would very likely to have provided her with private information that the good Judge would have preferred to remain exactly that. He was therefore likely to be unusually sympathetic to her entreaties.   I happened to know that it was Tregeagle who was on rota for judging for this quarter and not Jeffries but I kept that information to myself so that justice might prevail.

The journey via Truro had been uneventful and we arrived safe and sound at the Red Lion, St Columb's coaching inn and general headquarters for the town's Hurling team. A pleasant evening was spent with a few beers, some old friends and the timeless discussion of who got concussed and who did the concussing at the last Hurling match. The coach had been full as far as St Columb which meant that Isabella was fully preoccupied with intelligence gathering from the chattering classes. Departing from St Columb, it was now just the three of us. The journey promised to be reasonably uncomplicated. The prisoner's wooden leg had been discreetly detached and strapped to the roof of the coach. John Kneebone was not going to go anywhere very quickly.

I stretched out in the coach and prepared myself to sleep off the afterglow of the previous night's beer. As my eyes closed I noticed with some horror the look of concern and compassion that was starting to realign the chins and various layers of make-up that comprised the face of Isabella B.S.; an open invitation for master Kneebone to launch yet again into a tale of innocence and undoing. Then came the inevitable and fatal question.

'My poor man,' Exclaimed Isabella B.S. 'Please do explain what actually did happen to your leg when you were at sea protecting us from pirates and Barbary slavers?'

I prayed for it not to be the 'cabin boy and the cannon ball' or worse still the one about 'the captain's hungry crocodile'.

'Twas on account of my pibrek' responded Kneebone and I inwardly groaned. It was a well-known fact that Kneebone had been the instigator of shipwrecks and not the victim. Indeed the absence of his left leg was assumed by many to be the result of injury sustained by a fall whilst involved in the dark art of wrecking. Using cliff top lamps to mimic safe harbour lights was a favourite ploy of wreckers but it was not without risk to life and limb. Many a wrecker had slipped in the dark and received their just deserts on the rocks below.

'You were shipwrecked? Oh my poor boy' Consoled the mistress of complex corsetry, 'Please tell me more.'

'Pibrek not shipwreck' corrected Kneebone and our fate was sealed.

'Pibrek not shipwreck' repeated Kneebone 'Playing bagpipes. In Scotland they call it Pibrock in Cornish tis Pibrek. I was on Mount Folly, up to Bodmin, entertaining the good folks of the town for their Riding Day. Me pipes were full of the wind and fittee sounding when they Helliers came stanking across the Folly and arrested me. They said it was on account of me causing alarum amongst the citizens and scaring the dogs. Well, there was no actual people in sight or earshot and the dogs was not scared, their heads were raised and they was joining in with harmonies. It was me that was scared. They ol' Helliers with their kilts, gert boots and blue tattoos, were a real piece of trouble. I heard tell that are really the spirits of Celtic hunters summoned up by the Raggadazio, the town worthies, with some strange druid ceremony out in Halgavor mire. The Raggadazio use them instead of the Town Militia cos last year they got themselves as drunk as Perraners on the Riding Ale. The Helliers scat all the standings as they dragged me off the Folly.'

'Plain English!' erupted Isabella B.S.

'Sorry Mam. Knocked over the stalls' continued Kneebone, 'I tell you what. If you want to buy a nice piece of leather, that is place to go. Bodmin's finest and fresh up from the tanneries. Mind you they do stink a bit. Talking of which when those Helliers dragged me through the tanneries they didn't gag nor retch nor nothing. They don't breathe like we, I am not sure they breathe at all. Anyway we went past all seven tanneries on the way to the jail. Seven stinks for seven days apparently. They say each one has its own special character on account of the particular ingredients they use in their tanning pits. 'Tis said that it is something to do with what they feed their dogs, who, after all, provide them the one of the main ingredients for the tanning pits and give different colours to the leather. I have heard tell that the Guild of Wild Dogs has declared the Borough of Bodmin off limits for all its members cos of the strange food given to dogs in the town.'

When Isabella B.S. failed to pick up on this unlikely Guild I could not help but notice that her cosmetic fault lines were now tracing a mixture of anxiety and suspicion across her features. Her eyes were looking at the rather fine striations and colourings of her leather boots with deep suspicion. A suspicion clearly shared by her nose which was beginning to twitch.

'Well' continued Kneebone. 'We came to the Jail gates and I was fooched through the durns.'

'English, dear boy! English! What do you mean fooched through the durns?' admonished Isabella B.S.

'Sorry Mamm, fooched through the durns, shoved through the door posts. The stink of the tannery pits was gone thank goodness but now there was something else attacking me poor nose. There was a sharp smell of something hot and sulphurous like the very Jaws of Hell were opening. And then I saw the gallows. It made me shiver to see the hangman's rope swinging there, hungry for the next victim. It stood out against the black stonework behind it. So black it looked like a passage to somewhere darker and deadly. I shuddered and welcomed the next bit of foochin' across the yard and a final fooch into a small side room and the Court Clerk.

'Kneebone' greeted the Clerk 'Not vagrancy again! You should have had more sense than to go begging in Bodmin Town, Justice Jan Tregeagle's home patch and he will have no sympathy. Throw him into the cells until court opens boys.'

I protested that I had done nothing but provide honest entertainment but it was no good and I was back out in the yard dangling at the end of a Hellier's arm before my protesting of innocence was ever finished. And there was still that strange pungent smell coming from the gallows. The rope and noose were flicking like some angry creature's tail and that blackness seemed to be taking on a shape. Too much imagination and tannery fumes, I said to myself as a bit more foochin' by the Helliers sent me through the air and landing on a cell floor.

'You all right?' enquired a voice in the corner which it seemed belonged to a rather becoming young maid 'They can be a bit heavy handed those Helliers.'

Now I know from bitter experience that being in confined spaces with becoming young maids was as likely as not going to get me into even more trouble. I politely introduced myself and learned that she was called Ann (no relation to the judge) Jeffery.

'You're looking hungry' she says 'Tell you what - the Piskies are coming any minute now, they always bring a good spread to eat and there will be plenty spare'.

My worst fears about sharing a cell with young maids were realised. Any hint of Piskies mean trouble for me and any mention of them in my explanations and speaking out for clemency to be wasted effort.

For once in my life a fist grabbing the scruff of my neck and marching me off was welcomed. I waved goodbye to the mysterious maid and tried to ignore the little green apparitions now laying out her lunch. A bit more foochin' propelled me across the yard. There was definitely something strange going on. The darkness seemed to be slowly creeping around the gallows and oozing across the floor. The rope and noose were flicking even more angry like and seemed to give out a whisper.

'An eur a wra dos mes na wra dos an den!' '

'English man, English' interrupted I.B.S.

'Twas Old Cornish, Mam," Kneebone explained. 'Something to do with the hour coming but not the man.' and continued his tale.

Well I felt some cold and shivery. I felt even more cold and shivery when I was fooched into the courtroom and found myself in front of Justice Jan Tregeagle and the Raggadazio. Their faces were all leathery and misshapen, eyes and ears and noses all being where they shouldn't be being. 'I never done nothing wrong' I said ' 'edn't no vagrant - I was just playing me pipes'.

'Aha!' Bellowed Justice Jan. 'You are indeed spared the charge of vagrancy on this occasion but by your own admission you are guilty of far, far worse!'

There was a creaking noise and a musty smell as the Raggadazio stirred and variously muttered 'guilty', 'hang him', 'make an example,' 'an affront to decency'.

Well I thought that was me done for but the Clerk of Court stood up and says 'Your honour. Clearly guilty but what exactly did he do and were there any witnesses?'

Now Justice Jan Tregeagle is one of those people who sees and knows everything on account of his wandering eye. His right eye found the Clerk first and then nudged his left eye, the one that wandered, so that it looked at the Clerk as well.

'Damn you man - do you not listen? He is charged and found guilty of playing Pibrek on the streets of Bodmin without due cause and without license.'

'Um your honour' says the Clerk who was looking a bit wished by now, 'As a pint of ordure do we need some sort of witness or something before we find him guilty and hang him?'

 'Dam you. You are wasting the court's time. Fine - bring in the witnesses' commanded Justice Jan.

'Sorry your honour but the only witnesses were the town dogs who have since been ordered to leave the Borough by the Guild of Wild Dogs on account of the strange toxic substances being force fed to them by members of the Guild of Tanners '

'Guilds!' Exploded Justice Jan 'Guilds! Is the natural curse of justice to be diverted by the Guilds?'

The Clerk of Court did some thinking and then turned to face Justice Jan's right eye. By this time the left had lost interest and was wandering again. It had become taken with something black and sticky was oozing under the door.

'Perhaps we should call an expert witness from the Guild of Pipers your honour?' says the Clerk of Court.

There was a cough and a cloud of dust and mildew as one of the Raggadazio muttered something about all the pipers being up to Altarnon for St. Nonna's Ale. There was some more rustling as the effort of muttering had caused one of the Raggadazio's ears to fall off and it was now stanking across the floor all on its own.

'In that case we must summon Henric of Pydar, Piper to the Earl of Cornwall' shouted Justice Jan.

'But he's been dead for 300 years' says the Clerk.

'Zactly' shouted Justice Jan 'He won't be gallivanting up to Altarnon with the other pipers will he! Raggadazio you know how the summoning of spirits works. Get on with it!'

Now I could see things were really starting to go very wrong in the Court room. The Raggadazio shuffled into a circle and some more bits fell off as they drew some kind of Druidic sign on the floor and started chanting. The ear that had run off in the first place was now stuck in the black ooze seeping in under the door and attracting even more interest from Justice Jan's left eye. Justice Jan's right eye turned to the ghostly shape now forming in the Raggadazio's circle.

'At last some sense in the Courtroom' shouted Justice Jan 'Are you the Piper of Pydar and founder of the Guild of Pipers?'

The ghostly apparition slowly removed the bagpipes from its shoulder, glided towards Justice Jan and looked direct into his right eye. The judges left eye, however, seemed to be trying to attract the right eye's attention and draw it to the seeping ooze coming under the door. Only by now no longer seeping it was a great swirling mass of black. A hissing 'Yesss' came from the apparition although no movement from the mouth. 'Yesss. I am he but as you see by summoning me you have unleashed the beast!'

'It has to be said that I was afeared by the Raggadazio' admitted Kneebone 'And I was even more afeared by the gallows but now I was really, really afeared. The court doors were smashed open and a great hairy creature came out of the darkness. Hot, blood red, eyes it had and great paws clawing their way into the court room like they come from the depths of Hell. And the teeth, you never seen nothing like it, great fangs dripping with blood and that ear was now impaled on one of them. Now, I know what you are thinking, but no, I kept me legs tucked well in out the way and everything else tucked out of the way. The Beast was clearly intendin' to take to a bite of something and it wasn't going to be me if I could help it. Then this terrible voice come from out of the Beast "A wra dos an ur! A wra dos an tebelvest!"'

Kneebone was clearly in good form today and I readied myself for the inevitable 'English! Boy!' but I.B.S.'s attention was elsewhere as she delicately and carefully extricated her feet from what she clearly now recognised to be 'Bodmin's finest,' fresh up from the Tanneries' boots. And Kneebone's tale carried relentlessly on.

Well the Beast gave a roar such as I have never heard before and pushed first me and then ghostly piper aside until he towered over Justice Jan Tregeagle. The Judge was now all shaky like and got even more shaky when he was seized by those great fangs. The jaws of the Beast closed and it slowly dragged Tregeagle back towards the darkness which in turn gradually oozed back through the door.

Suddenly I felt something tighten around my left leg. It was that black ooze that had come under the door. It was twisting around me leg and getting tighter and tighter. Next thing I knows I was dragged across the floor, out of the court room and straight towards the darkness behind the gallows. Twas like the Jaws of Hell from they old Cornish Miracle plays dragging me further and further in. Just as the Jaws of Hell closed a fist caught me by the scruff of the neck and with a bit more foochin I was safe. Well most of me was, but my left leg had been caught and was now gone somewhere completely different.

'Tis all right boy' said the owner of the fist who saved me and turned out to belong to the ghostly Piper of Pydar. 'Sorry about the leg, but being the Jaws of Hell all the pain and puss and messy bits is on the other side. You're left with nice tidy stump and I know just how to fit'n up.'

With which he takes out a large knife and plunges it straight into my belly. Not my actual belly you understand but the belly of the goat me pipes were made from. He cuts a neat circle in the leather around the long bass drone and draws it into cup shape that perfectly fits the stump of my left leg. Next thing you know the bass drone on my pipes has become a fully adjustable wooden leg!

Well that is the story of my leg and there is not much more to tell. With Justice Jan Tregeagle gone no one was worried about my piping anymore and I returned to my travels.' Kneebone sat back with the satisfied smile of a job well done.

'Quite, quite Boy!' responded I.B.S. absently as she desperately rummaged through her baggage to find alternative footwear as the coach pulled in to St Bennets Abbey.

My day ended with a stop at the Jail to hand over Kneebone to the warders.

'Another customer for Justice Jan Tregeagle' I said as passed the prisoner over.

'Not Justice Jan' said the warder and I could not help but notice his kilted attire and blue tattoos, 'Family problems and he had to go away at short notice. No tis Judge Jeffries come back to take over for this quarter'. I winced as Kneebone winked at me.

'Well' I said 'This prisoner is to be tried for vagrancy'. The kilted figure turned to face me with cold dead eyes that sent a shiver down my spine.

'No' he said abruptly 'Plagiarancy not vagrancy. He is accused of plagiarism, of stealing our story'.

Author's Note:

The author is indebted to the Clive Little and the Raggadazio of the Bodmin Play for permission to borrow characters for this tale. John Kneebone was tried in his absence during a recent Raggadazio foray and found guilty of plagiarancy. In Kneebone's absence it fell to the piper in the play (the author) to suffer vengeance on his behalf.

The Three Times Kneebone Saw His Dead Wife and the One Time He Didn't.

Now, when I tell you that I've heard any number of fantastic tales from Mr. Kneebone I know you'll believe me, but rarely have I had the chance to hear four in a single go.

It was a fine day in late spring and a group of youngsters just out of their classes were wandering the streets of the town. They were of the age where the young men had started to notice the more 'feminine' attributes of their finer classmates, but the lasses wanted no such involvement. Three young ladies walked ahead of two gents, who by all accounts seemed more interested in pushing one another out of the way than in doing anything to ingratiate themselves in the hearts or even kinder thoughts of their companions.

As the crowd of them pushed past the old tree across from where I was standing, a whistle sounded, followed by a thunderous clap. Layers of muslin frilled about their ankles as the young ladies spun in surprise. Their companions luckily had the good sense to rush and survey the area from where the disturbance might have originated.

'My good sirs!' Kneebone bellowed in his own gruff way. Rolling to his side, what had appeared to be a pile of discarded cloth took the form of a supinated man. 'Perhaps you'd be so kind as to fetch me my leg?' His tone and intonation were clearly put on for the sake of currying favor. Kneebone made a broad gesture to an item laying a few meters away - his prosthesis.

The gasps of the girls at the sight our friend Kneebone sent the boys thundering to his side, fists raised, keening with indignation.

'Get gone, you old fool.' 'Roll away, if you can't walk.' 'Look at him, thinking he can talk to us.'

But did John Kneebone move in his own defense? Did he hide away with shame? No, he sat up from his grassy repose and watched as one of the young ladies gently retrieved his leg and as if floating on a gossamer cloud, carried it to him.

'Aye, there's a good girl. You've done me a kindness.' The boys had relaxed their aggressive stance and the other girls grouped tightly behind Kneebone's heroine.

The girl seemed a bit flustered, and as she turned away I realized that I knew her. Her family had attended the local parish before moving away a few seasons ago. My nature compelled me to reintroduce myself, and reassure her that Mr. Kneebone would do her no harm.

'Young Miss Chegwin…' I began as I crossed toward the group. I wasn't permitted to finish the thought.

'You remind me of my wife.' This caused the young lady's eyes to meet Kneebone's gaze. A blush crept over her cheeks as she looked away. 'But I'm not sure at all that she was ever as young as you. Ah, my dear departed wife.'

'John…' I warned, but he paid me no heed.

'Lamorna was her name. Conceived on that beach she was. She's been lost to me now for five summers. Too long.'

Now, I've met Kneebone's wife. I've met and toiled over and prayed for the whole clan of them. His wife was assuredly not dead. When this particular man starts to spin a tale, you can be sure he only has one thought in his mind.

'Oh you poor man, I am ever so sorry.' Yes, Miss. Chegwin was as kind as a girl her age ought to be but was seemingly bereft of common sense, and possibly propriety, as she stepped from the road onto the grass and delicately lowered herself, arranging her skirts as she sat.

The group of young people had gathered around him, but no one joined the pair on the ground.

'Yes, well. All that's left for me is to carry on and to be the man she wants me to be. Even now still she wants me to tread a good path. Heh, so to speak.' He chuckled as he slid his leg back into, well - his leg.

'Even now? Whatever do you mean?'

'My 'Morna, she told me a year ago how she wants me to live.'

'Daft bastard, you just said she was dead five years.' One of the young 'gentlemen' exclaimed.

'That she is, but even the dead have a way of reaching out from beyond the grave. Particularly when it's your wife trying to tell you what to do.'

'John…' But again my warning tone was not enough to stop him.

'Three times I nearly died myself, and three times her ghostly self saved me. On the fourth time, she taught ME to save me, and she left me this here reminder,' he said, thumping on his artificial limb.

Well, this had them. All of the girls were now seated and the gents had taken to leaning on a nearby tree. With a sigh, I took my leave but retired to a waiting bench just in earshot.

'Soon after I lost my Lamorna, I was overtaken by a powerful need. I found myself at the Anchor.'

'The pub? See, he's just a lousy drunk.'

'Aye, that isn't untrue young man. But this was more than just a need of spirits. I had been wallowing alone in my rooms for too long. Something compelled me to that pub in search of companionship, conversation, and diversion.

'But the moment I walked in, I knew that I'd made a mistake. The whole place reminded me of her. The smell of the malt. The sticky feel of the floor. It was all Lamorna. So I stayed. I soaked it all in. I reveled in it - in her. But the more I drank in her spirit, the more I was reminded….' he choked on his breath, and I rolled my eyes, '…that she was never coming home to me again.

'I'm ashamed to admit I had a few. And then a few more. Lord Above, forgive me, but I felt all at once that she was with me again. The ocean rolling in my gut felt like the first time I saw her. But before long, I found myself hoisted from my post and rolled out the door. I was staggering up Coinagehall, and no sooner had I made my mind up to turn around and take up residence outside of The Anchor, to just be nearer to where I felt nearer to her, then the rain started. Rain, thunder, lightning, all the aspects of heavenly rage. So what happened? Well, sure as I'm sitting here, in my staggering back to the pub I lowered my foot into the gutter, turned my ankle, and nearly drowned in the runoff.

'But that's when it happened. By the scruff of my neck, I was lifted. Before my eyes...dazzling; bright light and glory. Her form and face, as clear to me as if it was the day before she died. My 'Morna pulled me from the street. "That's enough John." It was all she said to me.'

Kneebone wiped a tear from his cheek. My vantage point was too far removed to be able to attest as to its authenticity.

'She pulled me from the gutter and from my need to drink. Her face at that same disapproving scowl as the night we were wed. I'd gone too far, and she pulled me back. Haven't had a drop since. She wouldn't want me to.'

The young audience sat in silence, unsure of how to respond. The candid level of this conversation what something beyond what they were used to.

'Ghost of yer dead wife? Not likely. Come on Chaps, let's leave this fool to his delusion.' A young man addressed his compatriots and stuck out his hand to assist Miss Chegwin to her feet.

'But of course,' Kneebone hastily spit out, '...that's nothing compared of the might of the magic.'

'Magic? What sort of Magic?' One of the girls asked; her fingers dancing over the cross at her neck. Kneebone had pulled the group back in.

'Well you see, seeing her so clearly and then her vanishing away as if a dream was as fraught to me as if she had died all over again. I couldn't stand the pain. But I didn't dare try to recreate the incident. She was clear; not a drop was to pass my lips.

'Now, I'm a good god-fearing man, but I know that there are some powers that he just won't allow, so I had to turn away. I visited well, I'll just call her the *cunning* Mrs. *Peller*. She gave me a charm, and taught me a dance, and turned me loose upon the Merry Maids.

'Well, there I was, wearing only what God gave me, hopping around inside that stone circle while waving a purse of cooking herbs in the air. I must have looked a right fool. And a fool I surely was, because again I slipped and was very well intended to smash the back of my poor tender head right on the arch of one of the stones. But you know what stopped me don't you?'

At first, wide eyes were the only response Kneebone received. The girl with the cross clutched it tightly.

'Your wife,' she quietly uttered.

'My blessed Lamorna, her hand on the back of my neck, held me inches above the rock that would have been my end. "This is not the way, John." was all she said before I found myself alone in that field again, sitting on the cow mess that nearly ended me. She told me that the ways of the conjurer would do me in. And now, I've devoted myself to our Lord. Attending services every day and twice on Sunday. A pious man is I.'

The girls now all sat with their eyes downcast, perhaps in silent prayer for Brother Kneebone. Perhaps repenting their own temptations. Perhaps just unsure of what to say to this elder of ill-fortune. The young men all seemed dispassionately unconcerned and ready to take their leave.

'But the danger!' Kneebone exclaimed, perhaps with a note of desperation. 'Oh, the true harrowing danger came some weeks later at Enys Dodnan Arch.'

This caught the attention of the boys. That arch, a natural stone formation set high over rough seas, pulled those to it who wanted to prove that they were stout of heart. Climb up it, swim through it, jump from it; prove you were no longer a child.

'Twice I'd seen her, and twice she'd told me that how I lived wasn't what she wanted. Well then, perhaps I could die correctly enough.'

Gasps of disbelief were sucked through gloved hands. The righteous Kneebone had attempted the untenable.

'The winds were in a wild state as I crawled up that rock face. It took all my strength and will to hoist myself up that jagged arch and over to the drop. I knew that as I fell, I'd hit my head on the wall, so I'd likely be dead before I'd even had the chance to drown. That seemed all right to me.

'My arms were torn and bleeding and my hair was whipped with the salt wind. I angled myself closer and closer to the edge, ready for my weight to pull me to my end. And then I felt it. The stone beneath me gave way and I tumbled towards my doom. But no sooner had I accepted that I had taken my last breath than once more, she did catch me.

'Lamorna held me in her arms like a newborn babe. Like the child that we had never been blessed with. She cradled me and set me gently back safely back where I had been, but away from the Enys Dodnan's edge. "It's not your time, my love," was the gift she left me. Then she was gone, and the foul wind followed after her. I lay on that rock until I heard the church bells, calling me home.'

Now, I can tell you that more than like, each of those boys had stood upon that rock, eager to test their mettle. They now all stood before this raconteur as white as sheets. How many of them had almost met their end at Enys Dodnan, I wondered. One by one, they sat on the grass. Perhaps too weak with realization to stand. Slowly, Kneebone inched closer to the assemblage. Speaking quietly, he bid them near.

'I had thought I perhaps would see her again. But now I know that I never will.'

'Why? You love her so dearly. Surely she'll reappear to you in the right circumstance,' Miss Chegwin protested.

'I tried. Truly I did. But the heavens held her back. You see, three times I misbehaved, and three times she appeared. The third time almost ended me. My Lamorna,' Kneebone sighed. 'She was as mean a woman as there ever was, but we suited each other. Then at least. I had to be nearer to her, so I went to the place that she held most dear. Her cove.

'I paid for a ride as far as the carriage would take me, and then I walked the narrow path down to Lamorna Cove. It was towards the end of daylight, and all I wanted was to sit on that shore and contemplate what she was trying to tell me.

'As I was ensconced on that rocky beach, I had barely gotten the chance to organize my addled thoughts before I heard it. Her voice. She was calling me, calling my name. It was coming from just up the beach. Something strange beckoned me there, as if from a thousand miles in the sky. So, what choice do I, a simple widower, have but to follow the siren call of my beloved?

'The voice gave way to a howling and strangled bark. What I had heard as my Lamorna's siren call, was a mutt being pulled out to sea. The poor beast didn't stand a chance. The 'tow had him and he was using every ounce of strength in his body just to tread the water. He'd weaken and drown in minutes.

'It was instinct, that's the only rational explanation. Unless of course, Lamorna pushed me, for the next thing I knew I was tramping into the surf and beating the waves with my two miserable arms, using all my force to get to that animal.

'Sheer will got me there, and got my arm around him, and got us both back to the beach. We lay there for a good bit; Staring at the darkened sky and willing our strength to return. Quite out of nowhere I heard someone say "That's enough. That's not the way. It's not your time." It took longer than I'd like to admit before I realized that it was me talking to furry Sir at my side.

'Another moment later, I realized that this was the first time since she'd died that I'd been in near mortal danger, and Lamorna hadn't appeared to rescue me. She didn't need to. I had saved my own self, and one of God's creatures in the process. I didn't need her anymore and I haven't seen her since. Furthermore, if I ever do, I'll know it means that I've gone down a path not meant for me. One that not she and not God wants me on.

'And here's the kicker; in the process of me fulfilling her wish for my continued piety and servitude, Lamorna saw fit to make sure that I was damaged just enough in my thrilling heroics that bloodletting could not cure the fevers placed by the gashes that the rocky cove had left on me leg. The surgeon had no choice but to hobble me. It's Lamorna's final gift to me, so I cherish it.'

'That's it?' One of the boys scoffed as he rose. 'This whole story and the ending is that you're glad you'll never see your wife again, and you're fine being half a man? I could have heard that from my father. Come on, let's leave.' The young men stood up and hurried away towards the shops. The girls lingered for a moment in consideration.

'Well, I think it's a beautiful story. May God bless you, Sir.' Ladies are generally much kinder in these situations, I find.

'Aye, he has already even today. Peace be with you.'

As the girls gracefully rose and departed, thankfully down a different street that their former companions had gone, I returned to Kneebone's side.

'Now John, what was all that?' I asked.

'Oh, just bringing a little light to the lives of the ladies, Sir.'

'I'm sure. You do recall that I know your wife and that she is alive and well and her name is assuredly not Lamorna.'

'Yes of course. Just a bit of fun. I was bored you see.'

'I can't imagine why. Fair enough,' I sighed. 'No harm was done. Take care of yourself, Mr. Kneebone.'

'Aye, that I always do,' he replied.

With a shake of my head, I turned my back and resumed my walk. But as I started I could not help but overhear the clicking of counting purloined coins and a jovial comment from our chronicler.

'Yes sir, that's enough. That's always been the way, and it's about damn time.'

Sally's Pasties

Today I was riding from Botallack to Morvah on private business when I found myself getting hungry. I don't affect too-refined tastes in food, as some of my friends who style themselves 'Gentlemen' do. I like the simple fare of our country. The one dish which, however, has always put me off is that concoction called 'Starry-Gazey Pie' which they serve down in Mousehole of a Christmas time. But it was early autumn, and I was nowhere near there.

As I entered Pendeen, a delicious aroma assailed me, from a baker's shop. I identified it as the scent of our beloved pasties and resolved immediately to stanch my hunger with the thing which was the source of this delightful odour.

I alit from my horse, and gave the reins, and a small coin, to a boy who appeared out of nowhere, it seemed. I entered the shop where, sure enough, a young woman (and a plump and pretty one as well) was just taking a tray of golden-brown pasties out of the oven.

'See here,' I began, 'I'd very much like one of those...'

'Sally!' Roared a voice from the rear. 'Av 'ee got those pasties out? If they burn, I'll burn ee with th' strop...'

This tirade stopped instantly when the baker (it was he, surely) stormed out to the front of the shop and beheld me.

'Oh- beggin' yer pardon, sir, I was just inquirin' if the girl here was doin' her dooty.'

'I quite understand, my man.' I replied, with a wink to 'Sally'. Such a complex task must be well-supervised.'

'Well' – he murmured, trying his best to judge my tone, 'The way the miners do come in and waste her time in gigglin' and winkin' distracts 'er, that's sure. Got to keep a sharp eye. Now, sir, what be your pleasure?'

I asked for a fresh pasty, and Sally wrapped it in paper. The little smile with which she favoured me, out of sight of the baker, assured me that she held him in no fear, and I predicted that soon she'd wed a Mine Captain and be out of that bake-shop for good. Lucky Mine Captain!

I took my dinner out to a bench in front of the shop and sent the boy to get me something to drink. My horse would no more run away than the baker's oven. As I sat, a memory started out at me, which I had begun to feel as soon as I heard the baker shout 'Sally!'

As I munched, I mused.

It was several years ago as I was taking John Kneebone from Bodmin Jail to Truro Assizes where he was to stand trial.

'Stir yourself, Kneebone, it's time.' Insisted the turnkey as he unlocked the pen in which Kneebone and several others were being held. 'Hands in the shackles. You know the dance!'

'All right, mate. I'm ready.' With surprising grace, John Kneebone hopped on his one leg over to the jail door. Once outside, his crutch (a potential weapon within the cells) was returned to him and he was chained to another prisoner. The turnkey herded the two of them into the back of the waiting cart I had brought to receive them and several others. I mounted the step into the cart, and sat where I was partly under the shade of the canvas cover which sheltered the prisoners and kept them unseen by all but the driver and, in this case, myself.

Up front in the open, alongside the driver, was a man whose fair skin and paunch, together with his fine clothes, made me suspect that he was not used to such transport and might very well soon be burnt by the sun, there outside the cover. It was no surprise that he was not in shackles. The driver cracked the whip, and slowly the horse began the long journey to Truro, with my own horse tethered to the cart, trotting behind.

I regarded the free man for a moment. It has been a study of mine to be able to infer, from outward observation, facts about a person. I decided to apply what skill I had in that line on this person. After a few surreptitious glances, I said: 'And you, sir. May I ask – as you don't seem to be one of those being sent to trial – how you come to be here?'

'I most certainly am not on my way to be tried!' he blustered. 'I am forced to accept this rude transport as my horse has suddenly gone lame, and I'm needed in Truro for a case.'

'As legal counsel?' I asked, thinking he seemed an educated man. I had taken him for a merchant, however.

'Not at all – as a witness for the prosecution!'

'In one of today's trials?' I asked, somewhat alarmed as he might well be about to testify against one of the men in chains in that very cart! Lucky it was that he and they could not see each other, and I could see them all.

'Yes, begad – in the case of one called John Kneebone! I saw him (the worse luck for me) cut a gentleman's purse in Launceston. A clear-cut case of the guilt of a common criminal. There's no doubt but that it was he. I had caught him at my kitchen door the day before, trying to flatter my wife out of some scraps and a cup of water. I sent him away with a cuff and a curse, you can be sure. And for this, I must leave my business and waste the day, and now probably tomorrow as well, sending the wretch to prison. I hope they transport him.'

At the mention of his name, I saw Kneebone bristle, and I swear his ears pivoted a bit to take in the conversation.

'I myself,' I offered, 'find that I must often interrupt my business to attend to such civic duties as this. What might be your business, if I may ask?'

'Baking, sir! Certainly you've heard of Minster's Bakers in Launceston! Mine, and my Father's before me. Finest breads, saffron cakes and pasties in the Duchy. Pray come and see me soon and I will load you with samples.'

I thanked him, though I had had the misfortune of sampling his wares already. Dry, tasteless things.

All were silent for a while. The clop-clop of the horse seemed put us into a trance. As we approached the town of Lanivet, John Kneebone looked over to the man shackled to him.

'Well, lad, what'd they get you for? Did you force yourself on some poor, defenseless maiden?'

'Something like that. My girl, Mary Beth, she was sweet talkin' with me. And we was carryin' on and she was pullin' her skirt higher and higher, and well, things just happened. Know what I mean? And later she starts havin' second thoughts, and she tells her Pa that I took advantage of her. And he gets in this mood, and he decides he's gonna get me. So Mary Beth and her Pa make up this story that it was all me, that she was took advantage of, and they go to the constable, and well, that's pretty much it. Here I am.'

Once he finished the story, things were quiet again for a while. Finally the lad looked over to Kneebone.

'So I told you 'bout me. What about you?'

'Never you mind what about me, my robin.' Muttered Kneebone, not wanting, I'm sure, for the listening baker to know that he was the very man against whom the baker was to testify.

'A tale deserves a tale, fair's fair.' replied the young lover. 'At least tell me how you lost your leg!'

Kneebone thought a minute, and shifted in the uncomfortable wooden seat. His expression changed a bit, and he rubbed his temple with his free hand.

'OK, son, I'll tell 'ee.' Kneebone replied, making sure to speak, this time, loud enough for the baker to hear, 'It was all about this woman named Sally. Now this Sally, oh she was a looker. Red lips always smilin' and kinda plump, you know, but in a nice appealin' way.

'We was living together, after a fashion, you know. She'd clean my clothes and cook my meals. And when I'd come home from the mine, she'd be there waitin' for me. Talkin' pretty and all. And I thought it was all pretty good, you know.

'But people told me to be careful. Especially about her cookin'. This one ol' lady from town, Hannah, she was kind of a hag. People called her a witch – I don't know. But Hannah says to me, "Tell me, John Kneebone, does Sally ever make pasties for ya?"

'I said "She does, I trow. She makes the best pasties I ever ate."

"That's fine, John. But tell me, does she put swede in them pasties for ya?"

"Swede?" I sez. "Didn't knaw ee was from Devon! D'ye mean turnip? Naw, I don't like turnip in my pasties. Just meat and tatties and onion."

"Well, good," Hannah says. "Whatever you do, don't let her put swede (or turnip, as he calls it, dear ob'm) in 'em. I'm givin' you fair warnin'. No turnip. Well, now you been warned. Follow that rule and you'll be fine."

'Well, I figured Hanna was sort o' crazy. What difference would it make? I remembered the warning, but that's it. I didn't do nothin' about it.

'And it were true. Sally made the best pasties in all of Cornwall. Moist and meaty and a golden crust. Yep, they was the best.

'So this one night I come home early. They closed the mine cause there was a storm comin' on and we needed to get home before it hit. So I get home and there's Sally, and she's makin' the pasties. Now right off I see this big ol' turnip and she's cuttin' it up for the pasty. Now I remember what ol' Hannah told me about the turnip, so I says "Sally, I'm not much for turnip. Can you leave that out of mine?" But Sally says it's too late – she already mixed the turnip with the meat and onions and potatoes. And that were it.

'Well, I was starvin' and the smell of them bakin' was wonderful, and me being hungry and all – well, they comes out of the oven and I dives right into my pasty. Et the whole thing. It was so good I ast Sally for another. So I end up eating both pasties, and there was turnip in both of 'em. Two turnip pasties in one sittin'. And I had a couple of mugs of ale with 'em and pretty soon I'm getting sleepy and before I know it I'm out.

'And did I sleep? For 2 full days, I just passed out. And when I finally woke up, I was in hospital in Penzance. I asked the doctor what had happened. And here's what he tells me.

'Seems they found me by the side of the road – all bewildered and scared as in a bad dream. And I musta been, mind, as I remember nothin' of it. They brought me to hospital and when I finally come to, I realized I only had one whole leg. The right leg. The left leg just weren't there – clear to up above my knee. Stitched up like a topsail, too. No explanation – it were just gone. You can imagine how I felt about that.

'So I ask the doctor and the nurses and all they can tell me is that's the way I was when I came in. Nobody had any answers for me. The doctor gives me a crutch and I started adjusting to bein' a timbertoe.

'And Sally? She uz gone. Nowhere to be found. So I goes into town and looks up the old witch Hannah, and tell her the story about the pasties and my leg and all. And Hannah just looks at me and shakes her head and says, 'I told 'ee, but 'ee wouldn't listen. And now I'm not sayin' no more.'

'And that was it. She walks away. Won't talk to me about it.

'But the very next day I'm in the garden pullin' carrots and this bloke walks up to me. I never seen him before. He looks down at my leg, and he shakes his head and says "Yep, jes like poor Will Trevarrow." So I says "Who are you, what are ya talkin' about and who is this Will Trevarrow?" Well, he won't tell me who he is, but he says I need to go see this Will – he lives over at Winnard's Perch.

'"What for?" I ask.

'"Just go see him. That's all I'll say. Just do it. Then you'll know." And with that he leaves, and I never seen him again.

'Now, I'm curious – what can it hurt? – and I decide I'll travel over and find this man. I convince my friend Eddie to hitch up his horse and buggy and take me over to Winnard's Perch. I tell Eddie I'll treat him to a pasty and ale if he'll do it, and he says all right.

'When we get to Winnard's Perch, I start askin' around for this Will Trevarrow. At first nobody knows who he is, but when I see the town blacksmith, I ask him and he looks at me.

"'Will Trevarrow." 'ee says. "Yep, I know him. He's the one-legged cripple what lives in the cottage just north of town on Mulberry Lane."

'So I follow his instructions and we find ol' Will's cottage. Will's there and sure enough, he's got no left leg clear up above his knee. So I talk him up a bit – he's a friendly, chatty sort – and finally I get around to askin' him what ever happened to his leg.'

"'Well, it were strange", he says. "I'm livin' with this woman, Sally was her name. She be spending time with me, cleaning the house, cooking my meals, you know, such as that. Lovely maid, plump as a pigeon and always cheerful. And she made some great pasties. Man, one pasty would make a whole meal. And then one day she says she's gonna make a special pasty. I see she's got a turnip on the counter, and I says 'Sally, no turnip for me. Don't like 'em. Just meat and potatoes and onion. But she shushes me away and says she's gonna make me the best pasty I ever had.

"And she does. Even with the turnip, it's the best pasty I ever ate. Delicious. So I ate 2 of 'em. Yep, it was wonderful. But pretty soon, I'm feelin' tired, so I goes upstairs to bed. And I sleep. Yep, the sleep of the dead. For 24 hours – maybe more - I sleep this deep sleep.

"When I finally wake up, and I start to get out of bed, suddenly I realize I don't have no left leg. It's gone, I'm telling ya. Right leg is fine, but I have no left leg. Clear up past my knee. It's gone.

"So I call out for Sally, but no answer. Nope, she's gone. Not a sign of her or any of her stuff. She's gone, and so is my leg. And that's about all I can tell you about it. No Sally, no leg. And here I am still hoppin' around on one leg."

Kneebone said to the young swain, "So all I can tell you is that somewhere in Cornwall there's a woman name of Sally, and I tell ya, whatever you do, don't eat no pasty from her. 'Nope, specially if you see a turnip around, you just run away on yer two legs as fast as you can."

The Launceston baker had listened to the tale from beginning to end, while pretending not to, of course. I guessed him to be a superstitious sort, for he grew rather pale as the tale went on.

I delivered my charges and Minster to the court, and, having business of my own, I mounted my horse and set off. I heard later, to my surprise, that Kneebone had been acquitted of the charges, due to the faulty recollection of Minster, the witness.

I found that odd at the time but thought no more about it until I was next in Launceston. I saw, in Market Street, a familiar figure coming toward me. Familiar, but looking haggard and unwell. It was Minster, walking with a plump and cheerful lady.

I greeted him, and we shook hands. His hand seemed damp and a bit shaky. I looked into his face and saw deep fear and worry.

'Lovely to see you again, old man.' He said. 'Squire Wearne, please allow me to present my dear wife, Sally.'

Nan Pedrick's Tale

I suppose that, reading these stories, you might think that Cornwall is populated mostly by men. Of course, that's far from the truth. Naturally, Cornwall has, as a substantial portion of its population, ladies. And thank God for them!

I don't speak entirely from a sentimental point of view. I, a married man, of course have feelings of a fond nature for my dear wife, and, in my youth, I was as likely to fall in love two or three times a week as any young man.

I mean that our society, like all societies, could not exist without the fair sex. As you notice, I did not refer to the female as 'the weaker sex.' I have learned from experience that there is nothing weak in the female character nor, any more than in the male, in a physical sense. Much of the good that has been done, and much of the progress that has been achieved in our land and in our time, could not have happened without women. And how would we survive, I wonder, if there were not a woman in each home to prepare the food (and to a large degree, grow it in their gardens) maintain the home, raise the children and do the myriad mundane chores which are necessary for the maintaining of a household and of a society?

I suppose that, given the chance for an education and the freedom to follow their own bent, many women would not remain long as domestic beings, but, if allowed, join the males in trade, science and industry. But they are not free. No more, I would submit, are most men free to follow their dreams and talents.

I have been lucky. I inherited from my father not a fortune, but enterprises that provide me with an adequate income. Properly managed, they can be passed on to my own sons, increased in value, when I go to my reward. Indeed, my sons are already very involved in aspects of my enterprises. But most men are not so fortunate. To be born poor is not very different from being born a slave. To be fated to labour in the mines, on the fishing boats or in the fields for the profit of others is very close to slavery. To live hand-to-mouth, dependent on wages which could stop at any time, at the whim of an employer or with the vagaries of the fortunes of industries and commerce must be terribly worrisome. Not to have a banking account with enough in it to see one through hard times is a prospect that frightens me. To be unsure that one can provide for one's family – horrible!

So we have the poor always with us. As an Overseer of the Poor in our Parish, I am perhaps more aware of the horrors of poverty and the inevitable link between want and crime than others who have the luxury of ignoring the human suffering and the degradation that poverty brings. Indeed, I am often viewed as a 'Radical' if I should happen to air my views in the hearing of some others of my station. Ah, well – If they had seen what I have seen....

But as to the women.

The most obvious example of how women are not the 'weaker vessels' that sentimentalists would portray them, here in Cornwall, are the Bal Maidens.

These are women, mostly, but not all, young. Some are younger women who are obliged to work until they can find a husband, some are widows or spinsters whose parents are dead and some are simply independent-minded women who have rejected the idea of being some man's domestic convenience.

They, the Balmaids as they are often called, are among the hardest-working individuals I have ever encountered. What do they do? Well – first, the word 'Bal' is from the Old Cornish, and means 'Mine.' These are women who work in the mines. Not as cleaners or cooks or what one might expect. They are laborers. As the ore is unloaded from the skips that bring it from the shafts, it passes over screens – iron bars, more like, that allow pieces of rock that that are small enough for the stamp-mill to pulverise to pass through to the conveyers below. The rocks that are not small enough are for the Balmaids. They, with hammers that many a grown man would be hard-put to heft, smash those rocks into bits small enough to be stamped and processed. This, of course, is back-breaking work, performed outdoors in both the summer swelter and the winter chill.

Miners, all men, down in the shafts and stopes, can, when it gets too hot – as it often does, especially at deep levels – doff their outer garments, and sometimes even more, until one might, on encountering a group of them working in steamy heat lit by flickering lamps and candles in an atmosphere choked by smoke and dust, imagine them the naked damned labouring in the deepest pits of Hell.

The Balmaids, of course, have no such option, even in the cruelest heat of the glaring sun. They must do their weary chore while clad head to foot in wool, with who-knows-what sorts of undergarments such as our society insists upon. They wear great wimple-like headgear to keep off the sun, as Lord forbid any of our fair Cornish ladies should be browned by its rays.

Of all of the ironic misconceptions I have ever encountered, the Balmaids make the idea of women as dainty and weak creatures, subject to fainting and 'vapours,' ludicrous. I have, in my experience here in our simple, rural Parish, seen enough of the life of the women and men who live here to know that most of what is popularly believed about the 'lower' classes (believed, at least, by the privileged classes) to be absolute nonsense and I wonder when our worthy – nay, noble – working people will demand a greater share of the wealth and dignity of our land.

I come now to the actual matter here and beg forgiveness for my ramblings. Recently I encountered a woman, well known to me, who has had as hard a life as anyone. She was married to a good man, a miner and overseer in the mines, and together they managed to put away a bit of money. This was a blessing to her when, sadly, he was killed in a mine accident as happens far too often. She, in her widowhood, ekes out a living from 'doing' for the finer ladies in the town (we have had her in to make some new curtains and other such jobs) and from careful husbandry of her nest-egg.

She, like so many others, has, on occasion, had the chance to hear John Kneebone spin a tale. Recently she was at our house delivering some cakes and such for a tea my wife was holding for some of her friends. I asked her what she remembered of Kneebone's stories.   Here's what Nan Pedrick said-

'This is the tale as I heard it, sitting with a glass of cider in my hand, in the famed Crow's Nest Inn. Now before you go accusing me of being a disgraceful maid, Mr. Wearne; for lolly-gadding about wasting her days in the shame of a Public bar, let me explain.

'The Landlord of the Crow's Nest, you see, had provided for us. Or rather his good lady wife, had, for she it is who firmly wore the trews in that house, from the moment she ran to drink the water at St Keyne's Well on their wedding day. By the "us" I mean the small group of perfectly respectable ladies of the parish, who like to rest their weary feet of an evening, once their visits to the market are complete.

'For a peaceful hour or two, without the direct company of our menfolk and their constant demands, and yet, within earshot of the company of men, as it were, The Crows Nest, has for us a Snug. A specially designed corner of the Inn, set aside from the raucous public bar, with comfortable benches and a warm fire, but nevertheless served by the bar, and within good earshot of all of the happenings and stories and the gossip.

'So our small group of women, Martha Watts, Sally Pearce, Old Betsy and myself, we would gather with our knitting and sit in the snug usually after market of a Saturday, and enjoy a quiet drink, and a bit of a chatter.

'Only sometimes, you know, we'd choose to sit in silence listening in to the conversation going on across the other side of the bar. The men in there often forgot our presence, as they wouldn't see us, and to tell truth, we've reached that marvellous age where we are invisible to all. So sipping our pot of ale, or glass of sherry, or porter, we'd cock our ears to hear the latest tale.

'Oh! I remember the time that Sally was horrified to hear her son Bert boasting of some conquest, and in a quiet moment she shouted across the room, "I'll give you conquest when I get you home Bert Pearce, conquest across your head with my pan, you cheeky little bugger!" Then for a day or two there weren't no gossip for us to enjoy as the men became guarded. 'But soon enough they forgot about us, and we could sip and knit and enjoy raising our eyebrows, or whispering to each other "What do 'ee think on that then Betsy?" For Betsy had lived a good long time, and seen it all.

'Now on this particular Saturday, we were heartened to realise that the old scoundrel John Kneebone was in the pub. I say heartened, because he do tell a great tale, as long as he is inspired, and all it takes for his inspiration is a stranger with a heavy purse. And, as it happens, although the Crow's Nest is a small public house, it is on the way between a good market town and a harbour, and as well as that, there are even sometimes folk from far afield who choose to stop in to get a sense of us.

'And so it was on this particular Saturday, that we heard the voice of a foreigner. All eyes were on me as the man asked for a pot of ale as I'm not beyond boasting that I have travelled. But no, I didn't recognise the accent. Kneebone, in his usual smart way, managed to put himself between the stranger and the landlord. With a loud groan as he exaggerated rubbing the top of his wooden leg, and an "'scuse me" as he asked the landlord for a screw of baccy to fill his pipe, Kneebone settled himself strategically.

'"Good evening sir," Said the stranger. "You must be a sea faring man"

'"I am that, but did not become one until I was quite old, for my old mother was so afeared that I might drown, that I wasn't permitted on pain of a good clip round the ear from her, to go to sea until I was able to reassure her that I could not possibly drown"

'At Kneebone's words, we in the Snug put down our needles, and looked at each other. We knew that John, the old scoundrel, was about to prise a pie and pint out of the foreigner, in exchange for a tale and the idea that Kneebone could not drown was a new idea to us.

'"You can't drown?" said the stranger incredulously.

'"Tha's correct. 'tis impossible for me to drown. On account of my leg."

'"On the account of your leg?" Said the stranger even more incredulously.

'"It's wooden." Said Kneebone giving it a dramatic tap.

'"But surely …"'

'"Nope, not what you're thinking. It's on the account of where my lost leg is that is the cause of my inability to drown. Indeed, my lost leg has saved me from the fear of ever drowning and if you'd be kind enough to buy me a bit of ale, and perhaps a pie, then perhaps I might feel the energy enough to tell you the tale."'

'The stranger was only too eager to provide Kneebone with food and sup; and it wasn't long before John filled his pipe, took a long sip of what had to be his third pot of ale provided by the stranger (who didn't seem in the least put out) and Kneebone settled back with a loud sigh and said.

'"Well! It was Martin Pascoe and me, who set out to do some what you might call unofficial independent mining over by St Agnes way. We were young men, and as I said, I had a yearning for the life of a sailor, but a mother who was stubborn and made me promise never to go to sea and drown; so I mostly spent my days doing odd jobs; this and that, mostly legal. There was this particular mine temporarily at a standstill. The cause of it being at a standstill, was that the local miners would not venture near it, after an old woman, Dorcas by name, had shown up at the mine ranting and bemoaning. Dorcas was distressed at losing her man to the mine, and although the local miners were sympathetic, a woman at a mine is an unlucky thing. Even the bal maidens know to keep a certain distance. And the men found the presence of Dorcas unsettling.

'"Then, one night, Dorcas disappeared and it was said that she had hurled herself to her death at the mine, and had consequently become a knocker. 'Twas too much for the miners. They refused to set foot in the mine after that.

'"You do know what a knocker is I trust? Do you have them in, is it - England - that you're from?"'

'For the first time the stranger sounded a bit peeved. "I do know what a knocker is," said he, with his hackles audibly rising, "And let us get one thing straight at once, I'm not English." There was silence.

"'Oh, beggin' pardon, you'm not Welsh for that accent I know.'"

"'No I'm not Welsh, but I'm every bit as much a Celt as you. And we have many freits concerning mines where I come from. I'm a Scot, sir.'"

"'Well then, sir!" said John Kneebone, "I 'm honoured to be providing you with a fine tale that I hope you can tell to your grandson in time, for you Scots are our cousins, and you are very welcome here!'"

There was a palpable sense of relief throughout the pub and Ol' Betsy smiled, and her expression of joy matched the murmurs of satisfaction coming from the other side of the pub.

"'A Scot! The man is a Scot! I've never encountered a Scot but I'm more than happy he's here!'"

'After folk had settled back, Kneebone continued. "Well, you know that both knockers and rats are the friends of miners. If you feed the rats, they will hang around as you work, and give you fair warning that something is awry, by running away when trouble is looming. And they say that the knockers will tap on the rocks, or even whisper at you, to give you fair warning to run if danger lurks.

"Well, Martin and I weren't frightened by the tales of Dorcas, and we decided to take advantage of the fact that the mine was being left unworked, and we headed out to do a bit of mining, in an unofficial capacity. Although the people we could sell to were quite official, and there was nothing unofficial about the money we earned. And I trust you'll understand, when I tell you that the mine owner lived a distance away, and was English to boot, so we felt no guilt!

"Ha! So there we were on our third day, and doing quite well. I was holding the pick and Martin was hammering, for we did take it in turns, but with every strike of the pick, I could hear what seemed to be a whisper "Jack -ee. Jack -ee."

'"I bade Martin to stop and sush, and bide a while while I figured out what was.

'"Then he heard it "Sounds like a woman's voice calling you by your boyhood name, Jackee." Said Martin

'"Stuff and nonsense!" says I.

'But Martin was getting troubled. He looked about and asked "John ...where be the rats?"

'"We then heard her again "Jack -ee ...Jack -EE!"

'"Oh no, no, no!" says Martin, "I've had enough!" And without a word, he downs tools and starts to run out of the shaft. I hesitated, see, I hesitated, because I don't like to admit to being afeared. I hesitated, and it was a few minutes before I began to reluctantly follow Martin. Then heard her voice loud and clear'

'"JACK -ee"

'"And next thing I know, well, a pillar started creaking, and soon the part of the roof came down and I was pinned to the floor. Well, I thought I was done for, lying there pinned by my leg, but Martin ran and found some of our buttys who were working not far away, and I got away with my life, but without my leg. I took a powerful long time to recover in me mother's cottage, but as I lay there bemoaning my leg, I came over all ansum and joyful, and didn't I laugh? I laughed fit to bust.

'"Old mawther," I says, "I can go to sea now, as I've always desired."

'"How you'd reckon that, boy?"

'"I promised to you that I would not drown, and now, I cannot drown! Zee, tis well known that when you lose a leg under the ground, that sooner or later, the rest of your body must join the leg. So I cannot drown at sea! When I'm ready to meet my maker; many years hence, I shall have to die close by ground at St Agnes!! And I don't plan to visit St Agnes for a good while yet! So I became that rare creature, the sailor who never fears to drown.

"'And although I lost my leg, I'm forever grateful to that knocker who called out 'Jack -ee' at me."

"'Now, d'you think that tale is worth another pint? And perhaps a screw of baccy for my pipe?

"'I thank you sir," Said Kneebone accepting yet another pot of ale. Here's a health to you. And may you grow old enough to have a grandson and tell him that tale."

'We four women in the snug, had sat silent, listening to every word, and finally glancing over at ol' Betsy, who had seen it all in her day. 'What do'st think Betsy?

"'Well, and dam and blast the man! Tis another tall tale that Kneebone have found in his travels ...for that tale I've heard before, about Dorcas the rare creature, a female knocker, who calls Jack-ee. But mind, fair play to him," she said with a satisfied laugh "...tis a fine tale for all that!"

The Captain's Pet

There are, in Cornwall, a number of illicit drinking establishments. These operate outside of the legal closing hours and cater mostly to the lower elements of society. In fact, some of them are associated with worse vices than drink, one of the milder of which is gambling.

There are, of course, some which are run by neighbours for neighbours – often these are called 'Kiddlywinks' – or just 'Winks' – for the practice, too often imitated in legal pubs, of adding a bit of stronger spirits, for which they are not licensed, into the beer of a patron who winks at the barman in just the right way.

I, of course, seldom find myself in any such establishments, as to be seen there could do damage to my reputation, and to participate in any of their worst vices would be my ruin, both in this life and in the Next.

On occasion, however, I have been forced, in pursuit of my duties as Overseer of the Poor, to stop into one of these places to see if a person living on Public Funds is throwing them away on strong drink, gambling or…. let's just say…. worse.

On one such visit, I spied, not to my surprise, a familiar figure at a table with several men I knew to be gamblers, and 'professional' ones at that. The figure's back was to me, but by his talk, and by the crutch that leaned against the wall nearby, I was in no doubt of the figure's identity.

I thought it odd that he was sitting where he was. At no previous time had I ever seen him sitting with his back to a door, as he was now situated. As I crossed behind him, quietly so as not to attract attention, I noticed that, at that time of day, someone sitting in that seat would have his face in shadow. Curious, I shook my head at the barman (he knew this to mean I would not be taking drink – he knew me well) and took a seat near enough to hear the conversation at the table nearest the crutch.

There were cards at the table, though no game seemed to be taking place at the time. The object of my curiosity was talking, which was no surprise.

'No, I fear that you gent'men would be too much for such an honest and innocent countryman as I. We are so poor 'round here that we have little to venture on the cards or the horses or such-like. I must save my poor earnings for my ailing wife and two infant sons, with the occasional bit of rum to keep up my spirits, and fear that what little I have in this pocket would soon line yours. No, mates, I won't play your games. I know only one game, in any case, and it may well not be known to you gents at that.'

'Not be known?' One of the sharpers remarked. 'Why – we'd be glad to learn it of 'ee, wouldn't we now?'

The others at the table nodded and grunted agreement.

'But I tell 'ee – I haven't the brass to make it worth your while. My poor purse….'

'Now do we look like the sorts who would take advantage of a poor, honest man – not to mention a cripple – like yourself? We'll keep the stakes low and be happy of the chance to learn a new amusement. Please – we're all agog to acquire the new game.'

I knew at that moment that all was up and that some kind of mayhem would follow. The word 'cripple' must never be spoken of my friend. He resented it deeply. Revenge would surely be his, and I began to gleefuly anticipate it.

'Very well, friends, I will try in my poor way to instruct you. And it occurs to me that as you have noticed and remarked on my lack of leg, a tale of it might be instructive, and partik'ly appropriate to our sitiation 'ere, veez a veez my skill or lack thereof as a gambler, and my lack of luck.

'The game is one I learned whilst on a French ship as cabin-boy, a lifetime ago. The frenchies call it "Poque." It 'as other names, I believe, but that's what I heered it called in those days. I'll mix up the cards like so. The "Shuffle" I believe you men call it? And I'll ast one of you to cut (is that right?) the cards to see that all is fair and propur.

'Now I'll distribute the cards – "deal" is the term as I recall it – I'll deal five apiece, although some deals seven or other numbers. Ye'll look at your cards and see what sense or combinations you can make of them. I'll recite for you the different names for the different combinations if you'll show them to me. If you don't like your cards, you can ask for other ones, discarding the ones you don't fancy. I'll replace them. You can only do that once, mind. Then, while you ponders your cards deciding whether you have a hand worth wagering on, I'll tell you the tale I had in mind. It will soothe you and make your choices easier. There's no hurry, y'see. We've got all evening to enjoy our game.

'As I said, I used to be a seaman of sorts. It wasn't only on that godforsaken French tub that I served. It lost me, its Officers and most of its crew as well as its sails, masts, keel and tiller to a Spanish warship on the coast of Floridee. That's in the New World, friends. Yes – I have indeed travelled to that great land across the Atlantic, although I travelled about only in the southeasternmost part, which seemed to me to be only made up of swamp and moskeeters, gents. And other wild and perilous game.

'Well – I didn't want to bide my time in those steamy climes for long, I can tell 'ee. It didn't suit my consteetution and I sickened somethin' dreadful. In the end I found a berth on a English ship – where they talk as near as they can to our proper speech and I could understand 'em. I took a billet as Cook, havin' some experience in that line, and sailed with them for – let's say a bit of a while.

'Now that ship was a bit of a maverick, shall we say. When I first went on board, I didn't think that much was amiss, but as time went on, I began to suspect that I had got myself into something I didn't expect. (That's called a 'flush,' pard. Not much of a hand. Most anything could beat it. Best not to wager much on it.)

I ast, early on, which port we were bound for. I ast this of a crewman, mind, and when he just gave me an odd look and laughed sort of dirty-like, I laid it to his native ign'rance and the common predoodice of English types against us honest and true Cornishmen. I thot little more about it (Now – that's a better hand, pard – better put down some brass) until I had occasion to be in the Capting's quarters servin' supper. I ast 'Where we bound for, Cap'n, Sir, if ye don't mind my astin?'

'Bound for? We be all bound for the gallows, my man, and don't you forget it! Haven't you realized yet what sort of gang you've joined? No? Well – just you wait until our colours fly aloft. Then the light may dawn in that thick Janner head of yours!'

'I waren't in no position to mind the insult, so I swallied it and went below decks to scrub pots and ponder. But I, in my innocence, couldn't fathom (if ye'll pardon the pun) his meaning. (Well – don't that beat all! I seem to have won that hand. Beginner's luck, I assure you, friends. Good thing the stakes are low, eh? And sir – Two pairs of any cards beats three o' the same. Ye'd do well to remember that in footyer. Bless me – I believe that I've won enough to raise the stakes a bit and to give you men the chance to win back some of this pile afore me. Only fair.)

'One day I heard some commotion above on deck. I was mindin' my work in the galley, cuttin' the bad bits out of the tatties and such, so I thought little of it until I felt the ship lurch sudden-like as we altered course more quick than called-for. I were no sailor-man, but I 'uz sure that no ship would do that unless at great need. As we weren't in no gale, needin' to cut about to crest a rogue wave or any such, the on'y thing I could think of that would prompt such a manoover was a fight! Not wantin' to be caught below decks during a broadside – again – but that's another story – I raced up to the main deck. And what a sight awaited me! (Why'd ye discard them cards, pard? Well – I guess you know what you're about.)

'Not two cable-lengths away, bearin' down on us like a hell-hound, was a ship of His Majesty's Royal Navy! She fired a shot from her bow-gun – as a warnin' I assumed – as it flew high over our masts – and, as I looked up to follow its flight, I seed what our Capting had meant by his kriptic ree-mark. Up there on the top of our mainmast flew the Jolly Roger!

'A cold sweat started in the small of my back, friends, as I saw that fearsome image – the grinnin' skull with crossed swords beneath. Some uses bones, but not our ship. Swords they were.

'I braced myself for the worst, and a watery grave to follow. But what do you suppose? (Ah – I've lost that hand. Well, my pile must reduce, friends, and yours increase. I'm afraid my skills as a gambler have… but where was I… oh, yes.) Our Cap'n barked some orders which were Greek to me, bein' a mere ship's cook and all and we sudden-like come about and seemed to be on a collision-course for the navy boat. At the last minute, though, our ship veered a bit and slipped just to the wind'ard of that navy tub. That quite lit'raly took the wind from their sails and made 'em tip toward us. Our gun-ports, it seemed, had been open all along and the Navy boys had not seen fit to open theirs on that side. As they opened them, their ship, as I said, rolled toward us with the absence of wind and they took in a lakeful of water through them ports.

'That of course drenched their powder and made those guns useless. Their lack of wind, together with our men reducin' sail at the right moment, made them a fish in a barrel for our artillery. We opened up on them and that side of their boat was reduced in an instant to mere flinders. I'll never forget the faces on they English sailors as they looked at the gaping rent in their hull, seen the water comin' in and realized that they were for the Locker.

'And they were, mates. They sank d'reckly and no attempt was made by our ship to rescue a man. Davey Jones and the sharks got 'em all.

'So now I knew where I was. I was on a pirate scow, and no way off. It were my lot, until I could get away, to cook for a crew of criminals and cutthroats. I resigned myself to my fate. (Oh – look! My pile has increased a bit again. And you gents seem to be picking up the game pretty well at that. Mebbe we should make it a bit more interestin'?)

I was to be on that pirate boat a while, it seemed to me. I learned that we didn't often stop in ports that normal ships frequented. There were some harbours in that Karribeen sea that catered to freebooters like us and had their own laws and customs. After visiting a few of those, I became familiar, to my 'ternal shame, with those customs. Sometimes to this day in a fever I remember some of those nights in port, soaked in rum, feeling strange fingers wanderin' over my frame, with the smell of opium in my nostrils. Yes, friends, those were sinful, shameful nights, and I'm glad nobody around 'ere knows I knew 'em.

'As time went on, I became familiar with every inch of that ship. Except for one bit. At the stern, below the Capting's quarters, was a room with a door with a big lock. It was, I heard, where the plunder from our thievery and rapine were stored. Countless riches abode there, was my understandin'. But what impressed me more were the sounds that came from that place. Sounds of something scrapin' along the floor, along with a sort of growl, hiss or cough that defies desript'n.

'At times, as we raided and re-plenished our fodder and water, we took on beasts, live and dead, which no human would eat. As cook, I was expected to butcher these, although nobody seemed to care whether I did it well or ill. When I asked what they was for, I was told only – 'The Cap'n's pet is hungry.' What that pet was, I could only spec'late, but I knew now what was behind that door, guarding that treasure. The Capting's 'pet' – whatever in God's green earth sort of monster that might be. (Now – see – when we're playing for higher stakes, you must be more keerful with your wagerin'. To lay down that much silver when you've got no more than a pair of nines – well - you see the result. I only hope that you new friends of mine may be fortunate enough to win back some of this undeserved stack before me. I'd hate to think I'd taken advantage of novices at the game.)

'One of the vices that those pirates could bring on board with them was gamblin'. They went in more for the rollin' bones than the cards, and I never had no luck at 'em. Being an honest man, I never thot 'till later that those dice might have been "loaded" as they say, to bilk a poor Cornishman and a sea-cook at that. No sirs, my poor share of the loot was soon in the pockets of my shipmates if I so much as looked at those dice. I became known as "Silverless" and that was my nickname after a few of those games.

'As time went on, and as I chopped up donkeys, armadillos and wharf-rats for the Capting's 'pet' I come to wonder more and more exactly what it was that was behind that door. I never was the one, I thanked Providence, to open that door and empty the bucket of stinking meat onto the deck inside that treasure room. That is, until, a few days after a stop in one port where there was sickness going around and most of the crew was down with a retchin' and bilious fever.

I had restrained myself from earthly pleasures that time, feelin' that perhaps it were possible to have too much of a good thing, and I were in fair fettle. We mostly drifted in the middle of the sun-soaked Carreebeen, hopin' to see no sails on the horizon. Bye-m-bye word came from the Capting that his pet must be fed, and I were to do it. I hefted a bucket of jackass parts, borrowed the key from the Quartermaster, and stepped aft.

'As I approached that door, I could hear the beast inside thrashin' around. It seemed to roar with rage and I quailed to put key to lock. I thought, though, that I had also heard the rasp of a chain across deck. Perhaps, I hoped, the monster was tethered.

'I screwed up my courage and turned the key. As I took the handle in tremblin' hand and pulled open the massive door, a thing rushed at me across the floor, only to be stopped, seemingly by magic but aksh'ly by a stout piece of anchor chain, inches from my feet. I took one look, threw the bucket and all in, slammed the door, twirled the key and ran.

'Soon after, the crew began to recover and life returned to normal. Except for being whipped for wastin' a good bucket (the beast had reduced it to matchsticks) I had no more to do with the Capting's pet except for chopping up vermin for it.

(It does my heart good, kind friends, to see your stacks increase. I had begun to feel awkward to have so much and you so little. Might I suggest a round of mild refreshment? The landlord's ale is gentle as a kitten and should in no way impair our play. Oh – damme – there goes the tic in my eye. Pay no attention to it friends, it's just a remainder from my days on that ship and comes on me when I think on them too much. But I'll carry on with my tale, as I've brought you this far. Pay no mind to my wink,

Jack, my wink d'ye mind, just bring us a round of beers. I'll have mine as usual in my mug that hangs on the peg there.)

'I'd had a good look, though brief, at the beast that guarded the loot. I knew, from knowledge gained in my travels, that the booty could have been no safer in the Bank of England. I had never heard of any attempt to steal from that hoard, but one. Rumour had it that, before any of the current crew were aboard, a foolish sailorman had slipped the key from the Quartermaster's ring as he slept and tried to sneak past the beast to plunder the treasure. The next morning, they found the door open, the beast sated and sleeping, and some bones and a foot that had been knocked out of the beast's reach. Nobody else ever tried it on, I was told.

'I have said that I was considered unlucky when it came to gambling (as seems borne out by the state of my current stack, sadly. Are you gents up for another hand? You seem sleepy. Another? Very well, I'll deal.)

'Ways were found to test my luck. We wagered (to pass the time) on cockroach races, on how many strokes of the cat o' nine tails it would take before a shipmate screamed, on how many ships we would spy through the glass in a day, and many such amusements. Sadly I lost most of those bets and my poor funds dwindled. In fact, as I lost more and more, I went into debt to some of the sailor-men of that crew, which, trust me, friends, you don't want to do. I was becoming desperate for a bet I could win.

'One day, it hit me. I mentioned just now, I believe, how I was desperate. I needed to be to even consider the bet that I began to conceive. One day, in conversation with the crewman who most often fed the Capting's 'pet' I happened to ask him what sort of beast it was, in fact. I knew full well, of course, but I counted on his English assumption that the Cornish are thick-headed to make my inqueery plausb'le.

'It's a crock, innit?' He said in his odd English way. 'A Crock – O – Dile' if you like!' Armed with this intelligence, I did, over the next few weeks, mention to every one of the men on board the Cap'n's Crocodile. Nobody argued or gain-sed me. But one. More on that later.

'I saw that I might succeed with my plan, and purposely began to get into deeper debt with my shipmates. I acted so fearful of those I owed that they made great sport of making threats on my life. Many a knife I had held to my throat in those days, together with laughter and deerission.

'Finally I felt that the time was right. One evening, after I had finished cleaning up and had served the Capting his port up in his quarters, I went down to 'tween-decks where the crew were loungin' and tossin' the bones.

"Shipmates" I said, "I am in debt to most of you, and fear that I may not repay you in this life. As you are all sporting men, I have no doubt that you will respect the terms I offer you on this last wager. With it, I bet my life."

'The room went silent at this. I continued. "I propose that I spend 10 minutes inside the door to the treasure room. If I die, I hope that you will consider that fair payment of my debts. However, I will claim ten times my debts to each of you from you if, in that ten minutes, I am not harmed in the least by any crocodile."

'Naturally, the room erupted in guffaws at that. I stood my ground, with an earnest face. Slowly it dawned on those men that I was serious and would do it. "Done!" shouted one to whom I owed a great deal. "And done!" Shouted another. "Done!" Cried a dozen more voices. And the bet was on.

'I was escorted to the door. As it opened, I saw the Cap'n descend the stairs to look on, wondering what the noise was about. A crewman explained the bet to him in basic terms, and the Cap'n smiled and nodded. I was shoved through the door and I heard the lock snap to.

'Now, I had not gone into this unprepared. On a shore stop a few days previous, I had obtained some of the opium that was so popular with some of the crews who frequented the dives where it was smoked. In the slops that were taken to the beast that day I had concealed a large gob of the stuff. Did I know what its effect would be on the animal? Did I know how much it would take to render him groggy or asleep? I did not, friends. That was my gamble.

'As it turned out, the dose I had given him was only enough to slow him down a bit. I managed to dodge his sleepy snaps and lunges for most of the ten minutes, though it seemed like hours. Until, at the last moment, it writhed around as I slipped on a bit of donkey-grease on the deck. As I fell, it grasped my left leg in its jaws and squeezed. I let out a howl, you may be sure, and the door flew open, that being the end of the required time. Thanks be to the Capting and his pocket-watch for ensuring fair play on the time. They pulled me out, but the "Pet" kept my leg for a late snack. They threw a painter around my stump and squeezed it to stop the blood, and later the "doctor" stitched it up as it is today.

'But what of the bet you say? I wasn't killed, but I had said, and I reminded the crew of this, that "I will claim ten times my debts to each of you from you if, in that ten minutes, I am not harmed in the least by any crocodile."

'"But you are harmed, Silverless!" The Quartermaster shouted. "Look at your legs – or can't a Cornishman count to two?"

'"Ah now," I panted in my pain and near-swoon "As to that, yes I can count to two. And I know one thing more. I was mauled by NO CROCODILE! That beast in there is – as I learned in my sojourn in Florida – a ALLIGATOR!"

'At this, the Cap'n broke out into a roar of laughter. "He's right, boys! Old King Looey in there is no croc. He's an alligator I caught as a fingerling in Florida and raised on this very ship. Pay up, boys! Lad, you're Silverless no more!"

(And so, friends, that's how my luck changed on the high seas. As it seems to have changed here. My, how you three do nod. I'm afraid that my tale bored you. Jack, would you help me to put these coins into a sack for transport? And please do keep a few of the larger ones for yourself. You've been admirably helpful this evening. In fact, in commemoration of this evening's events, I'll forevermore call this establishment 'The Lamorna Wink.' A good name, too. You should consider adopting it!')

The Landlord's Tale

As I have been collecting these tales, I have found that I am not the only connoisseur of Kneebone's stories. One evening when I was visiting a "local" in a town not far from Kneebone's past haunts I happened to mention my little project to the publican.

'Kneebone, is it?' He said. 'Many's the night I've stood behind this bar and gave ear to his lies. No matter, I thought, what's the truth in anythin' these days? 'Sides, it kept the maid busy pulling pints for him and his hangers-on, and I'm not against an extra copper or two in the till.

'But 'ere's the nub. I knaw the right of it! All the tales he's spun here and otherwise, and no doubt all the ones you've heard yerself (beggin' yer Honour's pard'n) are made from whole cloth and no more true than the Aprocrophilia (or so sez the Vicar.) I was there for a deal of it, and what I didn't see and hear for myself I've got on eyewitness testimony. What I know is gopel and you can bank on it!'

Naturally, I was intrigued. I wondered if this man actually knew the true story of the famous lost limb. Although I had been intending to make an early evening of it (I was staying in that same inn and my bed was just up the 'Timber hill' as the local folks say) I ordered a brandy and asked to hear the story. As the landlord began, I saw a few of the pub's patrons sidle a bit closer to hear, and a couple ordered more ale. Here's what the landlord said:

'It's not that John Kneebone was particularly pleased when he lost his leg; it still hurt, he said, and being able to feel your toes when you don't have any is enough to make a badger teasey.

'Here's just the way it happened. There were plenty of peglegs in the Wendron parish, even for a place with farming more common than seafaring. The tap-tap-tap on the cobbles often predicted the coming of an ol' sea Pollard - cast legless by a stray leadshot by a revenue cutter, a cannon from a French ship or an encounter with pirates from the outer colonies. Many lost a limb in the mines and spent their final years in the counthouses, dolling out meagre tributes to young men many of whom wouldn't live as long as them.

'Yet Kneebone's missing limb often brought laugher, scorn or fear to those who heard the tale. The tale of Kneebone's leg reached mythical status some years before, but now John was a hollow, haunted man his only friends were those who sought his company in bars like this to hear the tale.

'John sat in The Blue Anchor, over to Helston, nursing his fifth jar of Spingo. I was nearby, in the warmth of the fire, and the fire of the Spingo kept him warm and sedate. He looked out the window at the horses and hawkers; with pint in hand, the world outside seems so hard to understand. He tried not to let the visions of the real world interfere.

'He was slipping off the bench, so he pushed back with his remaining leg and perched his stump against the heavy table.

'Eyes and nods met across the table, grunts acknowledged and the tobacco-thick air curdled with camaraderie.

'Market day in Helston always brought out the characters, the crazies, the feckless, the chancers. John wondered where he fitted among all this. He wandered as well. His life was now a pity, travelling from market town to market town sleeping on floors and accepting charity from farmers, miners and fishermen all come into town to trade, yarn and generally get lashed up.

'Time was when John was at the centre of the bustle. Selling his wares, some ill-gotten, some genuine by the fruit of his labour. He was always seen as a scallywag, he was sly you see – big, sly and a knack for making money. Making money made you popular with the ladies as well. Yet money and ladies also made you a lot of enemies.

'John was saving, you see. He had had a plan. His cousins (by name, Sleeman) had got lucky in Canada, bought a bastard-huge range out at Bowmanville for next to nothing. Enough land for a family of 11 to live on and not see each other all day. That's where John was headed, away from the poverty, damp and wretchedness of his beloved Cornwall. He loved Cornwall, was a janner through and through – but, he had to get away.

'All well, until he lost his cursed leg.

'It wasn't the loss that did him in. It was the reaction after. Some people took him in, some scorned him. Some said the devil had struck him down for his ways, others said he was just unlucky.

'People mostly humoured John. Took him in, made sure he was fed and watered. They'd want to hear his tales, but the best tale was always how he lost his leg.

'Now… if John was a good storyteller, he was a better wrestler. In the days before he needed crutches, he was tipped to be a champion – a proper champion. Fame beckoned when he beat that Yannick Moncus when he was over from Brittany. Everyone reckoned Yannick was the best that ever put a sack on his back, but Kneebone had him in a hitch – and that was the end. Kneebone brought two acres of land with the proceeds.

'Pascoe was with Kneebone then, wanting to know about what happened up at 'Druth the past week. Hell-up in The London Inn, man got stabbed in the back.

'"Why," Kneebone pondered while watching the froth settle on this fifth pint of Special, "am I always where there's things going down."

'"Tell us 'bout yer leg, Kneebone," cried Boy Richards sitting across the way. Damn boy wasn't old enough be in 'ere, but he worked for Pascoe and market day was the one day when things could get wild. All good as long as you didn't miss church on the Sunday.

'John looked at Richards, and tapped his glass – yarns don't come for free. Richards, a labourer as he was, knew when respect was due and called for Sid the landlord to bring over a pint another of Special.

'As soon as the pint hit the table with a weighty thud, a silence settled in The Blue. Those who had heard the tale third hand got in close, those who had heard it from John's mouth before got in closer.

"'What 'appened was,'" said Kneebone dryly, "was diabolical. It was from the devil 'imself. When my time is due, when I go to hell and I catch Ol' Nick – I'll ram his teeth down his neck – just like I did to that pillock Yannick."

'A round of mirth softened the air, only to fall back in silence to await the next instalment.

"'We were up on Tregonning Hill, picking up the traps for rabbits and catching many more by the full moon," murmured John.

"'The night was quiet and it was just me and me lurcher, Joe, up on the hill. We had a good brace, enough for a fair shilling, and the air had changed. A soft wind was now behind us, anything uphill could hear us coming.

"'We should have stopped there, but I was greedy – too damn greedy. It's greed that makes you fail, not being in the wrong place. We headed up past the old burial mounds, the old fort walls and towards the quarry. 'Tis a place with history, but I knew it like the back of my mother's hand. If I was to be struck down blind, I would still know my way around that hill."

"'We come up over the round, creeping quiet and we heard a sound like we never heard before. Was like a hare dying, but hares had been poached out of Tregonning for years. It was a disturbing sound – like nothing on earth. I dunno who was passing tin more – me or the dog. We lay quiet trembling next to each other peering over the round, behind a gorse bush.

"'Then we saw it – the beast of Tregonning. It glowed a shimmering blue under the full moon; its thick coat covering a mass of muscle. Its eyes shone an evil green and dulled only by the rancid breath from its dripping jaws.

"'The beast was only a hundred yards away; you could hear its shallow gasps of breath and occasional snarl through the sabre teeth."

'The Beast of Tregonning was something of a wretched myth for anyone in the shadow of the hill. As much as people liked to scoff and scorn such notions of a giant hound with the head of a lion; there were too many sightings and deaths to simply pass the matter off as another tale to keep folks from poaching.

'Farmer Quiller had given up farming sheep up on the hill; their half-eaten carcasses almost bankrupted him and sent him to Bodmin. His son Zack still lived there, but never came out – some said Zack was mad as well. Then there was the sorry tale of Joshua Warren. He was just 17 when they made him dance from the gallows at Bodmin for the murder of Jessie Payne.

'Poor Jessie was a mere child of four-years-old when they found her body a mile away from her home at Carleen, in the footstops of Tregonning. Her poor body was laid to rest incomplete missing the head and legs. Joshua was the local simpleton and said he saw her last being carried away by a giant goat. They found blood on his coat that he said was from gutting fish but no-one defended Joshua. He said he never hurt no-one and cried out "Mother, help me" moments before the crack of his neck silenced the crowds who come to see him die. Joshua was odd, they said, but he wasn't a child murderer. What would he want with a young girl's head?

'"I knew then we were out of luck," said John after a gulp of his Special. "I knew then there was not going to be a good ending to this evening."

'John explained to the now crammed bar that he had had a plan. As hard as he was, he wasn't fighting no beast that night. So he decided to leave his rabbits behind, let the lurcher off the string and hoped that the beast would be done with the rabbits or chase the dog – he was certain Joe could outrun the beast given a decent headstart.

'"Joe ran wide, I threw the rabbits out by some gorse and dashed from mound to mound, half-crouched so much my legs burned in the night air.

'"When I heard the dog screech, I didn't look back. I didn't need to. I knew what had happened. I loved that dog and I didn't want to see the beast tearing its innards out. 'Sides, it was my innards I was more worried about.

'"I was nearly at the foot of the hill, just by the path to the road. I thought I'd made it, I did. No rabbit stew, but I kept my life. Then it all lashed up. I'd gone too far west, I didn't know this slope near Great Wheal Vor. The ground was rough as rats, and I was lurching all over the shop."

'It wasn't the pain that first made John aware he'd lashed up. It was the rolling and tumbling. He was falling, or rather rolling, into a dark space. His nails clawed at the wet rocks, looking for a way to stop his rapid descent. Then with a thud and a crack, John came to a rest. He was cut, bruised and at the bottom of a mine adit. That wasn't the worse of his worries; his femur was sticking from a gash in his pants. He'd broken his leg.

'John looked up and he could see moonlight through the adit entrance. The slope wasn't that steep, he reckoned he could climb up the slope. It would hurt like a bastard, yet he didn't want to die in a hole. Well, not at Carleen anyway.

'Aside from the pain, there was something else clogging his senses. A putrid smell of rotting, dung and urine.

'"I didn't know where I was," John said remorsely. "I knew I had to get out."

'John inched his way up the slope, away from the stench. There was death in that hole alright, every so often he come across some hide, bones of morsels of rotting flesh. He didn't question where the flesh was from, he didn't want to be part of the rot in a few hours time.

'The Blue was quiet now, even though a few more had joined. The laughter and mirth of market day had been taken to that cavern to die.

'"Then I heard that growl and saw the eyes," spoke John softly. "I was near the top and had one hand out the pit. I could smell the fresh air – but I could also smell the breath of the beast.

'"I froze with shallow breaths. The beast was not aware of me yet, I reckoned the smell had masked my scent. With luck the beast would leave his lair, and I would clamber out.

'"Just then, there was a movement outside. Someone was shouting. I looked up, then looked down – just to catch the beast's eyes glaring at me some feet below. I'd been found."

'John clawed at the ground and push with both feet, the pain from his broken leg causing him to scream. Just then, John saw a lantern and saw a stopped figure coming towards him. It was Zack, he must have heard the commotion.

'"I called to Zack, and Zack come over," murmured John. "I reached out to Zack and he caught by arm to pull me out. He pulled me out over of the lip of the hole and I thought I was safe, I really did.

'"But the beast was also there. The beast took my leg."

'John said that the last thing he remembered before the pain dulled his senses, as he lapsed into unconsciousness was his leg being shaken like a rag doll. He looked at Zack, and Zack was crying.

'John came to in Tom Thomas's house in Breage. The room was full of people. I was there, and even Rev. Geach was there.

'"Alright John, or no?" said Geach to a few laughs in the room.

'Yet not all took the joke. The forlorn faces told John that something was afoot.

'"When I come to," said John. "My leg was gone. Doctor Pascoe said there were teeth marks all over the place and he had to cut it off proper to stave off infection. There might be infection yet."

'"One day, mark my words, I'll go back to Tregonning and I'll face that beast again. One leg less, or no, I'm not scared. This idn't over yet."

'The Blue was quiet now, even a quip from Sid behind the bar asking if 'e ever went back to look for his leg and boot didn't lift the atmosphere.

'Those that knew Kneebone, and no-one west of Truro hadn't heard the tale one way or another, knew Kneebone wasn't a liar – a drinker, a scallywag, and a fighter – but never a liar.

'He would go back.

'The moment passed, people left the smoky alehouse, and more came in. John drank up the last of the beers left on the house, put a bottle of Special in his jacket and shifted his bulging carcass out of his seat.

'His pegleg tapped on the granite cobbles leading out of The Blue, as he made it out onto Coinagehall Street. The brightness (and the eight pints) caught him off guard, and he steadied himself on the doorpost.

'The town was emptying now, the deals were done – money earned, money spent.

'Kneebone looked out towards Sithney, there was just a couple of hours of sunlight left – he'd spent a few good hours in The Blue without knowing where he was kipping tonight.

'Then Ol' Trembath came down the street with his pony and trap, heading home.

'"Yew boi," John called out to him. "Any room for two on that cart, or no?"

'"Yeah, pard," said Trembath. "I'm going far as Breage."

"'Breage," that's fine thought Kneebone, as he uncorked the bottle in the back of the cart.

"'I can be at Tregonning 'fore dark…"

The last few words of that landlord's tale were still ringing in my ears as I went, weaving slightly, aloft. I had ordered a couple more brandies as the tale had unfolded. My senses and my apprehension were not at top of form, but a thought or two popped up in my half-sloshed consciousness as I laid my head on the spinning pillow.

One was that I knew, for a fact, even setting aside the inclusion of the mythical beast, that some of the things in that story could not possibly be true. The times, the dates, the people just didn't wash out.

Another thing that occurred to me was the increase in drinks sales that had occurred while the landlord held forth.

The last thing that I realized before sinking into a sodden sleep was that, in that barkeeper, I might have just met a more consummate liar and tale-spinner than Kneebone himself!

The Sea Witches of North Cornwall

Fishermen are among the greatest of stalwarts of Cornish working men. How many hours and days they spend, down by the bay, mending nets, patching boats and waiting for the cry from the Huer up on the headland of 'Hevva! Hevva! Hevva!' which means that he has seen a shoal of pilchards. And then the fuss and tumult! Each boat wants to be the first out so as to garner the greatest catch. Oars fly, men curse, a cloud of spray envelops their starting, and then a fleet of sturdy boats shoot at great speed to the fish, guided by the Huer on his lofty perch. When they come in, nets straining, the whole town turns out to help with the unloading and transport of the catch to the works where the fish are prepared – salted and barrelled – for shipment to Europe and the oil is extracted. I have often heard, in Newlyn, a fishermen's toast – a sort of prayer – 'Long life to the Pope, death to our best friends and may the streets run with blood!'

An odd thing, you may think, for good Protestant (mostly non-conformist) Cornishmen to say until you realize that the greatest customers for those barrels of pressed and salted fish are the Catholics of Europe ('Long life to the Pope') That the fish are the best friends of the fishermen ('Death to our best friends') and that the income from fishing will continue as long as the places where the fish are beheaded and gutted and all prosper ('May the streets run with blood.')

I have not spent as much time in the company of fishermen as I have in the company of other working men. My interests include investments in fishing operations, and I am entitled to 'The Boat's Share' of many a haul, but I have always been over-sensitive to the smell of fish. Not that the fishermen themselves are particularly odourous, but, in order to render their garments as water-tight as possible, they soak and coat them with fish oil. A fish-oiled jacket, on a sweating fisherman, is something I usually endeavour to avoid.

This once, though, I found myself of an evening in Paul. Across from the Church (a noble edifice) is a pub – the King's Arms – which is frequented by fisher-folk. I had some business with the Wardens of Paul Parish Church and was feeling a desire for some supper after. I stepped, therefore, into the King's Arms. As you will no doubt have already guessed, on this particular evening there was a familiar voice drifting over the heads of the regulars. I fairly crept to the 'Snug' and opened the serving hatch to hear, without being seen, what Kneebone was about to tell those hardy Fisher-Folk.

'Gather round, gather round. If you all keep me in rum and ale for the night, I will tell you an amazing tale.' Kneebone began. 'For here's a story you will never believe, but I tell you it truly did happen. I was up on the far north coast, in the fishing cove at Port Quin, helping with the fleet. It was there where I first heard of the nefarious activities of the Sea Witches, who served the coast from Bude to Trevose, or so the legend would have it.

'The East India ship Thornton was wrecked at Port Quin twenty or so years back along, and there was still talk about secret things that could be found hidden along this old Cornish shore. So up I went to this rugged old bit of coast, in part to work with the fishermen, but also to try to discover what secrets the East Indiaman Thornton's wreck may still reveal.

'It was in the first two weeks or so of my fishing exploits in the bay, that I heard of the old Sea Witches. The skipper of the fishing vessel I was on had mentioned them a few times and was obliged to call upon their services one September afternoon. It was a particularly quiet time due to a fine bit of weather, and the sails of the boat had received no wind for days. The fish were a plenty to be caught, but we couldn't leave the quay.

'Skipper called upon the services of Old Mollie, one of the Sea Witches of the district and I was amazed at the apparent effectiveness of her conjurations. Within an hour we had sailed on the high tide and was out in the bay catching a stiff breeze. The fish were very soon being netted and all was going well, and Skipper seemed to be controlling the weather by way of a length of knotted rope. One time the wind would be blowing, then it would suddenly stop, just when we needed to weigh anchor.

'Back safely in port, whilst at the tavern, I heard talk of an uncanny occurrence just along the coast, where an old woman had been conjuring the storms. There was a tale told sometimes, where a ghostly whistling woman was seen, and she was perceived as unlucky for sailors and fisherman. Her presence would often bring forth a storm so fierce that death would follow, and the superstitious said it was wise to stay away. What sort of place had I come to live in, I wondered?

'After a few more days of fishing with skipper and the crew, I became more and more intrigued by the tales of the sea witches, and I wondered if they could help me locate the truth about the East India wreck, as I was hoping to find at least something of worth for my stay in this salty old pilchard port, and I begged an introduction from the skipper, who became most obliging once a casket of rum was offered. Old Mollie, it seemed could be found in a cottage on the clifftop. This dwelling had far reaching views up and down the coast, from Lundy Isle to Padstow, and it was rumoured that she would light fires on the church towers in the vicinity to guide (or sometimes misguide) ships to safe anchorage.

'Mollie had also been employed as a Huer, but of late she had made a better living as a sea witch, selling the wind and making protective charms for the various boats based at Port Quin. Mollie though, was an outsider, quite typical of her kin, living on the edge of the village on the top of the cliffs. Visitors were not encouraged, and skipper reckoned I would best wait for her to next appear on the quay before any introductions could be made. In the meantime, I made some enquiries about anything that may have been salvaged from the Thornton wreck, maybe an old map or a trinket or two of some value. Of course, many in the tavern that night were only too willing to lend me their wisdom, and by the time I had left the establishment and neared my home I was ready for my bed.

'I found myself under a half moon in the sky and the tide was high. The sea was splashing over the harbour wall as I walked alone. The village was quiet and seemed blanketed in mist. The wind was blowing in off the ocean and the occasional boom was heard as the swell of the tide crashed into one of the many sea caves along the nearby cliffs. I could see my home when something unseen but powerful made me stop and listen intently for a moment.

'A faint song was drifting around on the wind, drifting around on the eddies, then fading before soaring again. It was the wind and the rum playing tricks I was sure. But then I saw movement ahead in the shadows, and without a thought I followed. Soon I found myself on the edge of the village and climbing up to the clifftop. A sweat was now breaking on my brow, and the half-seen presence leading me seemed to be slowing. I could see a dwelling ahead and the faint glow of what must be a hearth fire inside. I stealthily moved closer to the old cottage and edged towards the window. What I saw when I peered inside made my heart pound. Three women of varying age were sitting by a huge granite hearth, the scene was softly illuminated by the glow of the fire.

'On the table before them was an old wooden chest, and beside it what looked like two gold goblets and an old map, which the women seemed to be greatly interested in. They were pointing at various points on the map and talking in hushed, yet excited tones. It looked as though there may be other items in the wooden chest, but they were just out of view. What I could make out was an intricate pattern carved into the front of the chest. It looked like a labyrinth of some kind, and just as I was pondering the meaning of this, I noticed all three women staring right at me.

'I awoke with a start, and for a moment I felt like I had been running and stumbling downhill. But was relieved to find myself in my bed, with the moonlight softly illuminating the chamber. My head was aching with the afterglow of rum and ale, and I thought of the very strange but realistic dream I had awoken from.

'The following day, once our fishing boat had returned safely to harbour, I decided to walk up the cliff path. I wanted to see if the old cottage in my dream was real. The wind was still blowing across from the sea, and as I approached the clifftop, I recognised the path from my dream. And shortly I came upon the old cottage. In the daylight I saw that its roof was freshly thatched, and the walls were built from rough slate with granite lintels. As I approached the front door. I noticed a large piece of dressed slate leaning against the wall, on it was carved the swirly labyrinth design I had seen in my dream the night before.

'I knocked on the door and waited. No one seemed to be home, so I looked through the window. I could see the table before the hearth, as in my dream, but instead of the wooden chest and gold, there was a huge pale candle flanked by two large sea shells, which had been placed very precisely in the centre. However, there was no one home.

'There were several outbuildings scattered around the clifftop dwelling, so I decided to explore these instead, not wanting to feel that I had wasted my time in coming here, though my curiosity was now well and truly roused. The first building I entered was an abandoned and very empty pig sty, but whilst inside I noticed another, larger building beyond. I quickly made my way to this and as I entered through the old stone archway I saw the wooden chest that had stood proud in the old cottage on the sea witches table in my dream. As in my dream it was carved with the same labyrinth design that I had just seen outside the front door of the cottage, however, the chest was completely empty. I looked around the old stone barn, there were a couple of old wooden cartwheels, which had seen better days, and various objects hanging on the walls and strewn about the place, which caught my attention due to their unusual nature. There were fish bones in the shape of saws, bits of old antler, dried lobster claws, sea horses and star fish, fish egg sacks and lots of lengths of old rope and fossilised sea urchins. There were other unrecognisable artefacts here too, alongside lengths of dried stalks with yellow flowers. But one thing was clear, this was a working store room of unusual collectibles.

'Suddenly, I felt a real urgency to leave, so I left the building and made my way back to the cliff path. The howling wind had dropped, and the sea was calmer now, and as I made my way home, I wondered where Old Mollie, the sea witch, had gone. I knew she was active, as skipper had recently done business with her. It was back to the Tavern for me, I decided. I was thirsty, and the company of others had very quickly become very appealing.

'Drinks at the harbourside inn were very welcome that afternoon, and no more thought was given to sea witches and dark dreams. The raucousness of my surroundings and my fellow sailors brought comfort and ease to my mind. And for a few days it was back to fishing, and preparations for the ports first pilchard catch of the season kept me busy. All was steady and work-a-day, until the night that the full moon rose above the wooded hills and valleys that guarded the landward approach to Port Quin.

'I was preparing to settle down for the night, as I saw the large blood-red harvest moon slowly rise over the wooded valley to the east. It was a lovely, but eerie sight casting long dark shadows towards the village and filling my bed chamber with radiant moonlight. I fell asleep quickly due to the local ale, and before long I was once again in a vivid dreamland, where all seemed more real than my waking hours….

'The path to Devil's Hole where a small collapsed sea cave and sandy cove are accessible, snakes its way through tangled woodland and water meadows before reaching a craggy valley, whence a sparkling stream bubbles and flows toward the ocean. It was here that I had been led by the sea witches to discover some of the lost cargoes of the wreck of the Thornton.

'The views along the coast were long and clear, and the old fortified gathering place on the Rumps promontory, rumoured to be the sacred meeting place of the sea witches, was clearly visible across the bay. The sun was hanging low over the sea on the western horizon and the tide was low. As I made my way down the precarious rocky path towards the sandy cove, I thought I could hear voices from the beach below.

'A soft murmuring was rising on the sea breeze, and as I drew closer I could make out female voices singing a beautiful song to the sea. These ethereal voices made me ever more determined to get to the beach, and I soon found myself climbing across the last of the rockpools and craggy foreshore to reach the ocean-washed sand in the near perfect cove. Towards each side of the beach were lofty cliffs of dark stone and as I walked along the tideline, towards the sounds of the sea-song, I saw a deep cavern in the cliffs, which had collapsed sometime during the past, which had left a huge circular hole in the cave's roof. This was the place I had come to see.

'I awoke at first light with the dream still vivid in my mind. I was due at the harbour, and as I made my way through the village in the coolness of a September dawn, I noticed a bigger gathering at the quayside than I would have expected. Skipper was right in the centre of the gathering, alongside him was a woman, who appeared to be trading items from a large wicker basket. There was general excitement in the air, and as I drew closer I realised that this was Old Mollie, selling her charms on the quayside before the many boats sailed at high tide.

'As I walked past, she looked up and looked directly at me and smiled. I purchased a lucky shell charm and spoke briefly to Molly. She seemed to know all about me, which I found surprising and quite disturbing, though later I realised that loose talk in the Tavern would probably explain some of her knowledge, but not all of what she said to me. She seemed to have intimate knowledge of my dreams, which simply could not be explained. However, it was clear that she wanted to meet me at the Devil's Hole, at midnight.

'Later that day, I whiled away a few hours in the Quayside Tavern, before setting home to make ready for my midnight meeting. A squall was heading in from the sea, and dark menacing clouds were drawing close. Across the bay I could see the flicker of dancing lights on the Rumps, an old headland cliff castle, known for hundreds of years in the ancient Cornish language as *Din Pentir*, and wondered if the Sea Witches were responsible for the brewing storm?

'The tempestuous clouds continued to blow in from the ocean, and before long the seaward horizon disappeared in a blur of mizzle. If I was going out to the Devil's Hole for midnight, I would need my wits about me, but I was sure that Old Mollie was about to reveal where the wrecked East Indiaman "Thornton" had cast off her precious load.

'The turbulent rumbles of thunder brought my attention back to the task in hand, and I set off into the dark night and climbed up to the cliff-top path which would ultimately lead me towards the Devil's Hole. Crashing thunder and forks of lightning flashed ominously above the raging sea, briefly illuminating the scene, and I could hear mighty waves crashing on the sand and shingle beach far below. The tide was ebbing, and for that I was grateful. It was going to be a rough and messy night, but I was sure it would be worth the trouble to gain the trust of Old Mollie.

'The path on the cliff edge was dark and uneven, but as a seasoned traveller, I was used to picking my way through the gorse, heather and ragwort and it was mostly a well-worn track. The constant growl of the sea kept me company, and I soon found myself above the rocky cove that was home to the vast collapsed sea cavern of the Devil's Hole. Another blazing blast of lightning illuminated the beach below, and I began my descent, navigating my way through the huge craggy rocks, many of which stood like tiny islands within their own miniature oceans.

'As I cleared the vast rubble of the upper shore, I found myself standing on firm wet sand. The roaring surf was at its lowest ebb, and I walked towards the western end of the sandy cove, where the spectacular Devil's Hole collapsed sea cave was sited, forming a deep recess into the dark scabrous cliff. I could just make out the rocky entrance, thanks to another thunderous bolt which crackled and sizzled, plunging to earth from the grim savage sky. The storm was very close, and the air was thick with static and adrenaline. I could see a flickering light shining from somewhere deep within the cave, beyond the collapse. I called out, and a light was raised up.

'The thunder was sounding thick and fast now, and lightning was flashing every few seconds. During one fierce burst I spied Old Mollie sitting high up on a rock at the far end of the cavern, she must have seen me, as she climbed down and began to make her way towards me. The cave felt like it was shaking as the thunder was finally upon us, echoing around the dark sea-stained hollow. Torrential rain began to lash down, and was pouring in through the Devil's Hole, adding to the eerie stormy cacophony.

'Mollie was standing close now, and was trying to make herself heard, she was shouting something to me, but all I could hear was the menacing rumblings of the vast thunder storm, which now sat directly over the cave. I thought I heard other voices too, and briefly sensed other people close by. Then an almighty explosion of sound and light let rip directly above the hole in the roof of the dank cavity, and as I looked up I saw Mollie raise her hands and cry out. I ran towards her and pushed her out of the way as a mighty fall of rock and mud crashed to the floor of the cavern. I felt a hefty pain in my left leg, as it became buried under the remains of the cave and then all went dark.

'I came to on the wet sand, with the sound of the rain and the waves crashing together. I was surrounded by six men and seven women, one of whom I recognised as Old Mollie, as she held her lantern, so the men could assess the damage. I was in immense pain, and before I passed out for the second time, I heard one of the assembled say that my left leg was completely crushed and would need to be cut off.

'The following day I awoke in the upstairs room at the Quayside Tavern. I felt pained and dishevelled and was immediately offered more rum and beer to ease my sorry plight. The pain of having my left leg removed just below my hip was hard to bear. Still, I was told that I had saved Old Mollie from being crushed and was now a hero among the fishermen, farmers and sea witches of Port Quin. I drank more rum, and as I placed my tankard back on the bedside table, I noticed a small leather pouch close to the pitcher of rum.

'I reached out and gently eased it open. To my astonishment I saw that within the pouch lay a large shimmering diamond, so beautiful and pure, that for the briefest of moments I forgot my pain.'

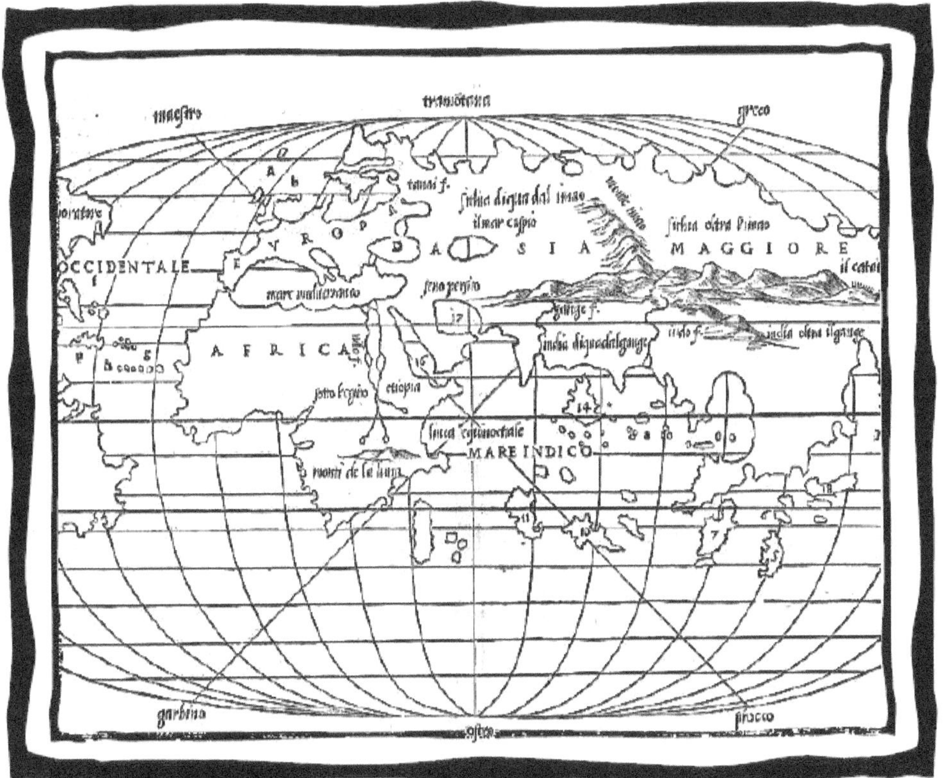

I have many friends among the gentlemanly class. I don't hold myself a Gentleman, as it is incumbent on me to engage in commerce as a means to a living. A true Gentleman engages in a Profession or in Trade only as a pastime. His Practise, his Living, his Chair are simply ways of productively occupying his time. Sadly, there are also far too many men who, finding themselves in no need to labour to earn their bread have it handed to them on a silver, or perhaps gilded, platter. I know but few of those, not being able to stick their company, mostly, for long, nor, I suppose, they mine.

Among my friends is a "Gentleman Doctor." He is a fine physician and has done much to further the health and well-being of the people of our mutual country, Cornwall. He is much admired and respected in the Duchy.

So much so, in fact, that I have had to conceal his identity in these pages. The name below is not, in fact the actual name of my friend, but his is, I can assure you not only as nobly Cornish a name as you will find here, but one which you might very well know or have read of.

When I began in earnest to collect the tales of John Kneebone, I supposed that those I had heard myself would suffice. As you have seen in this collection, many, as it turns out, originate from others than myself. This is a result of my having mentioned my little project to various friends and acquaintances and their being taken with the idea of contributing.

I never expected, when I happened to mention this project over a glass of port to my Doctor friend that he had ever even heard of John Kneebone. Imagine my surprise when he began to relate a tale. I begged him to write it down.

He chose to write it in the "Third Person." Here is the result-

'The wooden leg was indeed irreparably broken.

'It belonged to the old sea-dog John Kneebone. Whilst interned in Bodmin jail for some trifling infraction of the law it appeared that he had suffered a most unfortunate accident. Somehow his wooden leg had got caught in the mechanism of the treadmill and from that day the mill could not rotate. A technical investigation revealed that the mill was completely and irreparably deranged. No one had ever proved it was a deliberate act of sabotage, but the unfortunate prisoners, including poor John Kneebone himself, were deprived of the pleasure of their eight hours of daily exercise on the mill. But as a consequence, released at last to the sunny climes of the Duchy of Cornwall, John Kneebone was, as often the case, legless. Yet somehow he had cadged rides on various coaches, farmers' carts and even a small boat, and had made his way to the historic market town of Helston.

There, as bold as the brass nameplate, he had knocked on the door of Nicholas Penberthy, M.D.

Inside the wood-panelled surgery the good doctor looked sympathetically at the remains of the leg; less so at its owner. In fact he was aghast at the semblance of humanity that claimed it. Above the splintered remains were breeches of unfathomable horror, stained into rigidity with salt, tar, food, beer, gun-smoke, spittle, tobacco, ash, blood, snot, sweat, and the product of every human orifice. The doctor recoiled across the room, his head spinning. Clasping the table for support he cautiously advanced once more.

With considerable distaste he surveyed the owner of the breeches. The disreputable figure was of medium height, his face was as wizened as a walnut and much the same colour. His thick, black hair was uniformly greasy and was tied into a neat pigtail, rigid with a gruesome combination of solidified grease, tar, salt water and sweat. His hands were horny and strong but showed no sign of any encounter with soap or water. The nails were black with grime and possessed a distinctive, oily sheen. His sailor's jacket was curiously faded, though the sleeves were blackened with tar, and it was fastened with a cocktail of broken buttons, none original. The aroma of this repellent figure was strong and undeniably reminiscent of rotting fish.

But the wooden leg was crushed and splintered in two places, it appeared to be incapable of bearing weight, and it looked beyond repair.

The doctor's instinctive response, more a matter of survival than professional conduct, was uttered in one swift breath, "Mr. Kneebone, a new leg will cost three guineas. I don't suppose you have three guineas do you? Thank you, goodbye."

John Kneebone showed no sign of movement. He gazed patiently but soulfully at the ceiling. A salty tear trickled down his cheek. His lip trembled.

"It's hard being a loyal servant of King and Country. Defending his lands and his citizens through thick and thin, especially thick. And with just one leg too …"

"Yes, thank you, three guineas."

"An' my darlin' Jinny run off with some darn furriner from Tavistock, an' took my savings an' all."

"Three guineas."

"Not a roof over my poor head."

"Three guineas."

"But, do you know, for you, a good Cornish doctor with a historic Cornish family name, if you say three guineas, then that's easy. For a gentleman like you I'll pay up with pleasure. In fact, I'll gladly make it four guineas for your best job."

The doctor looked simultaneously both surprised and disappointed. Surprised at the offer and disappointed at the continued presence of his evil-smelling visitor.

"Well, I …"

"You drive a hard bargain. All right. Five guineas, that's my final offer."

"Tell me where did a shellback like you get five guineas? That's a year's wages I'll be bound."

"Money is nothing to me. I've won an' lost a fortune a dozen times over. But I can't be doing without my leg. Proper hysterical that leg is."

"Historical?"

"Zactly. Been roun' the world fifteen times."

"I'd have thought a simpleton like you would have believed the earth was flat."

Kneebone was indignant, "Of course not, no proper sailor wud ever think that."

"So, you believe the earth is a globe then."

"No, that's a load of rubbish too."

"I'll wager five guineas you're not going to tell me it's an oblate spheroid."

"Thank you, sir, I'll take the money. Of course, that's what they tell 'ee in school. But I'm afraid that's jus' the school answer, it's not the full story."

"Well if it's not flat and it's not a globe and it's not an oblate spheroid, then what is it?"

"Five guineas."

"Oh, very well, here you are. Now tell me, what is it?"

"A cylinder."

"A cylinder?"

"You heard, a cylinder. Stands to reason. The earth can't possibly be flat. If it was flat how would the sun get around to the other side? It's got to be cylindrical so the sun can go round it. All sailors know that's how "noon-sights" work. All us old-timers know how to use a sextant. Four minutes on the marine chronometer equals a degree of longitude, doesn't it?"

"Er, I expect so. But wait, wouldn't that also be true if the world was a globe?"

"I'm afraid it can't be a globe. Simple geometry shows that."

"Surely not."

"Five guineas."

"Oh, all right."

From a battered satchel Kneebone produced a salt-stained chart of the world.

"This is a proper sailor's chart," said John Kneebone, "Made by my old shipmate Gerard Mercator in 1569, see it's got his name on it. Sailed the seven seas with him I did. Now most people look at a chart like this an' they think the world is flat and square, just like the chart is. But that can't be true. Listen, my first sea captain was the Greek shipping magnet Aristotle."

"Don't you mean magnate?"

"No, magnet, he always pointed north. Well Aristotle noted that during a lunar eclipse the shadow of the earth on the moon is curved. That's the curve on the end of the cylinder. Right?"

"Er, if you say so."

"Now you tell me, seven days before it's full, what does the moon look like?"

"Half a disk."

"Very good. An' seven days after it's full, what does the moon look like?"

"Half a disk."

"Zactly, I can see you are a man of intellect. On those days the shadow of the earth on the moon is a straight line. It's because the cylinder of the earth is then at right-angles to the sun's rays."

"Oh, I never thought …"

"Bless you Sir! Now you know! An' this 'ere chart is just a miniature representation of the cylindrical earth, spread out flat. Have you got a ruler?"

"Just a moment. Yes, here you are."

"Now then, put your finger on the chart. Imagine you are down on the equator and on the Greenwich meridian, what's that gulf called?"

"Guinea?"

"Why, thank you, Sir, that makes it eleven! Now imagine we sail off through the sky on a heading of 45 degrees east of north. Go on, you lay your ruler on it. Where do you pass latitude 45 degrees north?

"It's at longitude 45 degrees east."

"Excellent, you are quite right."

"Now jus" you look at the chart. Where do reach reach 90 degrees north?"

"It's here, at 90 degrees east longitude, north of Siberia."

"Exactly, we'll make a navigator of you yet."

"Now imagine we are back at our starting point on the equatorial meridian. By that gulf; remind me what wuz it called?"

"Guinea."

"Oh, you are too kind! Thank 'ee, that makes twelve. Now imagine that this time we sail off through the sky on a heading of 45 degrees west of north. If the world is a globe we should finish up at the same place."

"Indeed."

"And where do we pass latitude 45 degrees north?"

"At longitude 45 degrees west."

"We do indeed, we're travelling at right angles to our previous course."

"Now look again at the chart. Where do we reach 90 degrees north?

"Why here, at longitude 90 degrees west, north of Alaska."

"Zactly, on the opposite side of the world. 180 degrees from that other place north of Siberia. Now what's the diameter of world?"

"About eight thousand miles."

"So these two places are eight thousand miles apart."

"I'm not sure …"

"Look, what is the angle between 90 north an' 90 south?"

"180 degrees."

"Zakly, I knew you wuz a man of education. Think of your basic geometry. 90 degrees is a right angle an' 180 degrees is a straight line. So the earth must be a cylinder, otherwise 180 degrees wud be a curve."

"I'm still not sure …"

"Bless you, of course you're not sure, you've been indoctrinated all these years. But this map proves it. Cylindrical projection it's called, because the cylinder of the world is drawn as a flat chart."

"But, that assumes …"

"You should believe me. The only man I couldn't teach navigation wuz blind."

"Blind? How did he lose his sight?"

"His foot got caught in a bight of the halliard. As we hoisted the sail he got hoisted by his heel, and when he wuz upside down his eyeballs fell out!"

"Really?"

"It's a well-known phenomenon. It happens in pigs."

"What?"

"If you suspend a pig by its tail its eyes fall out. Only certain breeds, mind you."

"Saddleback? Old Spot?"

"No, those small hairy pigs. Like a hamster?"

"A guinea pig?"

"That's the one, that's thirteen by the way."

"But that's a child's joke."

"Forgive me, I couldn't resist it."

"All right, we'll call it twelve."

"But I've been lucky. No accidents or injuries at all."

"But what about your leg?"

"That wuz quite natural. It's a common sailor's problem. It's called evolution.

"All living things adapt to their environment. In winter the hair of the hare is white so it can hide in the snow. Same with the ptarmigan, it has white winter feathers. Well mankind is the just the same. When we get old an" start to feel the cold our hair turns white."

"What about those men that are bald?"

"Rich people. They spend all day by the fire, they have warm clothes. Nature tells them they don't need their hair so it falls out."

"But what about women?"

"It's written in the good book, if a woman should have long hair, it is a glory to her: for her hair is given her for a covering. King James said so in his Bible, an' we are all loyal servants of the King, aren't we? You're not one of those republicans are you?"

"Oh no, no, of course not! But what about sailors' legs?"

"I wuz coming to that. To get to Australia we head south an' east. We have to, the winds are from the west. So the wind comes over the starboard rail, we are on starboard tack most of the time. The boat is tipped to port. So over time, to save all the 'ard-working sailors from toppling over their right legs grow shorter."

"But what about the return journey?"

"Well, like I said, in Australia there's a special place where we all 'ave our wooden legs adjusted to work on port tack. It's called the Gulf of Carpentaria."

"But Sir Francis Drake, Sr Walter Raleigh, they didn't have wooden legs."

"Ah but they wuz officers, Captains even."

"So what?"

"Being officers, they spent all their time sitting down drinking port and sherry. Their bodies had no need to adapt to life at sea. But us true workers, we have evolved to become the magnificent nautical creatures we are."

"Look I have a very fine leg here, let's try that on your stump."

"Thank 'ee, sir."

"Let me adjust the straps for you."

"Oh no! No, no!"

"What's the matter?"

"I don't suppose you got this from a returning sailor did you?"

"Well actually that's right. How could you tell?"

"And I bet you paid a pretty price for it?"

"Yes, I did."

"Then I'm very sorry to say you've been fooled."

"How?

"That returning sailor was a trickster, a con-man."

"The leg looks fine to me."

"It's useless, completely useless."

"What do you mean?"

"I told you, all proper sailors get their legs adjusted in Australia before setting out on the return voyage. You've been sold an Australian port-tack leg, but all British sailors need starboard-tack legs. This is just scrap wood in this country."

"But I never thought …"

"Look I feel really sorry for you. This is a total professional embarrassment for a good man such as yourself. Tell you what, just give me a guinea and I'll take it off your hands. I promise I won't breathe a word to anyone."

"But a great sailor like you could take it to Australia and sell it there."

"Half a guinea?"

"Done."

Kneebone picked up the leg and the twelve and a half guineas. He marched to the door with surprising agility, and as he left he shouted, "Just think about it. If it's a cylinder it can stand on end without toppling over. If it wuz a ball it would just roll away!'"

Pisky-Led

As a good Churchman, I don't hold with all of the things that the old people say about the 'Old Gods' and 'Druids.' It seems to me to be just a mixup of old tales and superstitions and as I am, as I said, a member in good standing of the Church of England, I mustn't give credence, or even listen to such stories.

Having said that, however, I confess to sometimes feeling my skin crawl or seeing the hair on my arms stand up straight when I pass certain places at night, or when a shadow passes over a full moon. We Cornish are bred to superstition, I suppose, and I, as a true Cornishman, cannot claim full immunity.

Here in Cornwall we are rife with reminders that, long ago, such stories and legends were the stuff of life and the very religion of our distant ancestors. It's said that we Cornish (and the Welsh, I suppose) are descended from the very ones who first peopled these islands. I have heard tales, in fact, which suggest that when our forebears first came here, they walked from Europe into an unpopulated land, and, where we now find the formidable British Sea, there was only a wide valley with a stream running through it.

Those old people could not, of course, have known of Christianity. They had their own gods, spirits and ghosts with which they peopled every crack and crevice, every peak and vale, every moor and hedge. No place was without its other-world guardian or demon.

Miners especially were prone to superstition. This was most prevalent once they started mining underground and no longer scraped tin from the surface, or 'streamed' the tin from excavations made through the fields and the peat to reach surfaces of long ago onto which the tin flowed in long-buried rivers.

Once they started to mine down in the hard rock, the creaks and cracks they heard, the seeming muttering that was sometimes just out of hearing, the lights they sometimes saw where there was no-one to make them started a whole new school of explanatory tales and customs intended to placate and appease what they felt to be malign forces and spirits who lay in wait for an opportunity to lead a miner down a false tunnel or to drop rock from the roof of the stope onto his head. Or, at the very least, to blow out the candle on his hat and curse his matches so that he had to grope, perhaps for miles, in the absolute dark, with horrors racing through his mind, back to where he could find light and company.

Others had their ways as well – I'm told that no fishing boat will go to sea with a woman on board, or a pasty. Imagine a burly fisherman being afraid of a pasty! Mind you, I can easily imagine any man, fisher or miner or farmer or even a Churchwarden, being afraid of a woman!

Farmers, being utterly at the mercy of the elements, gave to those elements personalities and bodies. There was (and is) no end to the ways in which farmers seek to placate the gods of storm and drought and ensure a good harvest. And when the harvest has been good, to perform the rite (a favourite of mine, though I am obliged to view it as simply a folk ritual) of 'Crying the Neck.'

There are many, even in these days, who put much weight in these old ways. In many villages there are women, and some men, who might, were it not dangerous to do so, call themselves Witches and who are well-versed in folk healing techniques and apt to distribute blessings (and curses, I fear) on their neighbours.

In Penwith there is a stone with a hole in the middle which is said to have many powers in the line of curing disease and removing curses. Many a Cornish infant – and adult – has been passed through the hole in that stone.

But what has this to with the subject of these tales? Where does John Kneebone enter into the picture? I do not suppose for a moment that he believes in the old ways and stories any more than he accepts the Truth to be found in Scripture, may the Lord have mercy on his soul. But no matter is too obscure, too strange, but that Kneebone could try at least to use it as a way of trying to wheedle a drink or a coin out of the unwary.

I am slightly acquainted with a family who lives far out on the moors. They eke out a miserable existence through farming (of a sort) and have a small flock of sheep and some chickens.

They are of the old ways. I have often tried to get them to come to Church, even offering to send a waggon to collect them, as the nearest house of worship is miles away. But they refuse, and persist in their belief in pagan spirits, gods and ghosts.

Once, as I was riding across the moor, I realized that my horse had had a shoe come loose. This was not uncommon on the rough and rocky paths

I was obliged to ride on my rounds as a Warden as well as in pursuit of my own business matters.

I remembered that the father of this family of moor-dwellers, whose hut I was near, was a passable farrier, and decided to visit him to see if he could re-shoe my horse, as well as to check on the welfare of the family. I dismounted and let my poor mount, now hobbling badly, walk without my weight the last half-mile or so to the squalid shanty where the family dwelt.

'Aye, zquire, I can mend the shoe.' Said the ragged paterfamilias. 'Step ye inzide and she'll gi' ye a dish of tay and a bite. T'other man won't mind.'

Imagine my surprise when I saw 't'other man.' It was no one else but John Kneebone! He greeted me effusively and enthusiastically, as was his wont, ever eager to ingratiate himself with Authority, as trivial as my authority was.

As I settled onto a dusty seat, and as the Lady of the House fetched me a cup of murky 'tea,' I realized that Kneebone had been relating a story.

I had, as you are aware, heard many of his stories, and he knew it. I had never (well, hardly ever) attempted to challenge or debunk his tales in the past, so, it seemed, he had no hesitancy in launching himself, despite my presence, into a new one for the benefit of the family – and, I suspected, for the benefit of himself in the form of a pallet of straw for the night, and an egg for breakfast.

As it would be some time before my horse was fit to ride, I settled back to enjoy this tale of Kneebone's, and to be entertained by his invention and his skill at crafting a tale to a purpose.

Here's how it went, to the best of my recollection.

'….and, as I was sayin', down in Penwith, too, the fogs can roll in sudden-like and thick. These aren't just reg'lar fog such as you gets up 'ere on the moors. These is sea-fogs and have got themselves up a good head of steam (pardon the joke) as they blow up across the Isles of Scilly and on-shore at Lan's End.

'One day I was travelling on foot – or on feet, I should say, as this was while I still had two – and had occasion to cross some fields and pastures away down by the very tip of our sacred Duchy. I had ben enquirin' of work at the Ding-Dong Mine and, finding that they didn't require any hands at that moment, thought I'd head off to Trewellard to see a mate.

'The weather that morning was fine, so I thought I'd go cross-country. I knew (I thought) every pebble in every lane and every stile in every field down those parts. And so I did, in daylight or under a moon at least half-full. So I set out.

'Well – I pointed my nose toward Trewellard and started following it. I worried a bit when the wind shifted inland – a bit early in the day, I thought – and the whisps of fog started catchin' themselves on the odd gorse-bush and bramble. But I didn't mind, and pressed on, thinking of the warm welcome and brown ale which awaited me at the Trewellard Arms.

'Things began to get a bit dim, mind you, as I trudged along. I missed a stile or two where I thought they ought to be and it took some looking to find them again. In fact, it may well be that I mistook one for t'other. I soon found myself in fields I didn't recognize, with only mist on the horizon and no landmarks to guide me.

'I pressed on toward what I b'leeved to be forrard. As I went, the fog kept closin' in the more. I had a nasty turn as I sudden-like spied something looming afore me, a vast hulk, it seemed, blocking my way. I moved forward carefully, and soon saw that it was no more but the biggest rock in the Nine Maidens! Then I knew at least that I was on the right course, and that there was a path nearby, where the farmers bring their cows back to skyber for milking.

'I found the path and figured that it was smooth sailing from there. I went on, and let my mind wander, thinking that my feet could find their way without my help. After a bit, however, I felt that I had veered to the left a bit too much on that path and determined to cut cross-country again for a bit. I found a stile on the right side of the path, next to a gate, and clamb'red over into the pasture.

'Well – by now the fog had closed in propur. I could see mebbe 20 feet in front of me, and all the world, except for the rough grass at my feet, was a white mist. I didn't slow down much, though. I kept on the way my unerrin' instink toward food and drink guided me.

'I didn't slow down much… until…'

Here Kneebone paused. That in itself was unusual. His gift of invention was so quick and spontaneous, he usually ploughed straight through his stories from beginning to end with no let-up and with a gleam in his eye. His pause, and a slight change in tone, made me glance up at him. He stared down at the table, and no light was in his eye. He looked, if anything, frightened. I had never seen him look so, and it drew my attention, you may be sure.

'Yes, John,' I prodded. 'Until…'

He looked up, with an odd, vacant look, at me. Then down at the table again.

'To be sure, Squire. Sorry. I just had something in my mind for a moment. Where wuz I…?

'Oh, aye.' He went on, albeit slower, softer and in a different tone than I had ever heard from him.

'Oh, aye… I started across pasture, y'see. Again, I could see nothin' but mist, and it were getting darker. Was evenin' comin' on already? Were the clouds bankin' up above the mist? I couldn't tell. My mind seemed confused, somehow, and I didn't know the time o' day.

'As I stepped on, again, something seemed to be in my path. Another stone, I thought, and I was right. Not a stone like the one afore, but one that stood up alone, thin and tall, carved as square as a support beam in a mine. Just there, in the field with no companion nor company.

'Well, I was beat. I looked at that stone, trying to recognize it, for a long time. I lit matches to see if there were a arrow on it and the name of a town. There were letters, or marks dug into it, I could see that, but in what heathen or devilish language I couldn't tell. And from wandering around that stone, trying to make it out, I was so twisted-up I didn't know whence I came, or where I was goin'.

'I stood stock still. A clammy chill seemed to be draped over me. I could see dark patches of mist blow, like clouds in a iron-grey sky, over that pasture. Sometimes I could see almost to where I thought the fence should be, and sometimes I couldn't see my hand before my face. And I could hear things. Not things like you'd expect. Not the sound of cows callin' to each other along the path to barn. Not a farm bell callin' the men in from the fields. Not even a ship's bell rounding the Cape.

'I heard, or thought I heard, voices. Snatches of talk, and bits of song. Couldn't make out a word, but they were voices, I swear. Almost like children's voices, so high and light, but seeming to say things that were both grave and merry, both deadly and comic, all mixed up. And sometimes they said my name. In spite of the strange, cool air, I began to sweat.

'"John!" They said. "Havee lost thyself? Which way is the pub now, John? You'll never find it, y'know. We've got 'ee now, and we'll keep 'ee if we wish!"

'Well, at that, I felt sick to my soul. I didn't know who these folk were, but they knew me and could see me, and damned if I could see them. I knew that I were likely to die or go mad if I stayed, so I ran.

'By now, it was full dark, though I didn't know the time. I could see no more than a miner who'd lost his candle. But I could see lights. Here and there, points of light blurred by the mist. I ran toward one, but it ran away faster than I could follow. I tried again with a couple more, but they either went off quickly, went out, or flew up into the air. I ran and ran, in a blind panic, until I fetched hard up against the wall of the field.

'That knocked me over and winded me, you may imagine. I picked myself up and, as I was leaning against the wall touching my head to see if it bled and trying my limbs to see if they was broke, I heard another voice.

'It wasn't like the others. It sounded propur Cornish, it did, and was high pitched, but not in a ghostly way like the others, but more like the little man who came once to Penzance with the circus.

'"Well, John," it said, "Us 'ave had our fun with you, y'know, and it's time to do you a service as payment. Lemme lead you a while."

'"How can you lead me when I can't see 'ee?" I asked. "Show yerself!"

'"I'm right 'ere, you ass. Can't you see nothin'? No, no – down 'ere!"

'I looked down. In a soft, blue glow that he seemed to make hisself – there was no sun or moon to make it – there stood a little man. No bigger than a child of two or so and dressed in old-fashioned clothes. 'Who be ye?' I asked, with a lump of fear in my throat.

'"You know that very well, John, and you know as well that if I were to tell you my true name, you'd never see hearth nor fire again, but wander these mists forever, getting smaller and smaller, older and older, until you'd be no more than I am.

'"For I've been on these Moors since before the Britons came. My sorrows began in the Ancient Times when the first boats came up the coast, full of cruel men with whips and slaves at the oars. My word of advice, John. Never beat your slave. At least not so much that he dies. Unless you like this mist and darkness enough to want to live in it forever. But enough. Time to get you out of here."

'He bade me to put my left hand on the wall and to follow his voice and glow. He set out at a quick pace, scampering and twirling as he went. I stumbled along and saw his glow dart to the right. Soon I met with the corner of the field, where the wall went off at a right angle. I turned and followed, figuring that the gate and stile could not be far off. After a while, another right-angled corner. Still I followed his glow and his mocking voice. "John – you sluggard – keep up or you'll be lost forever!" He called to me. Another corner. I came on it so quickly that I ran into it but didn't lose my grip on the wall. I could see him far ahead, glowing and flitting, but heard no more voices.'

Here Kneebone began to pant, as if he was running, even though sitting at the table, staring blindly at his cup. There was a mist of sweat on his forehead as he went on, talking quickly and as if to himself.

'I ran on. Another corner. I ran and ran, not seeing his light at all now. Another corner. I stumbled. Where was the gate? How many corners had I turned? Another corner. Surely I must have missed the stile. I must go 'round again. Or had I gone around twice already? I panicked and took my hand from the wall to run faster. Another corner. Another. I ran and ran and…

'It was light. The sun shone bright and clear. The mist had gone, and it was morning. I lay in a heap, aching in every joint and bleeding from my head and hands from blows and scratches gotten in my flight. My clothes were torn, and my shoes were missing. In a few moments, warmed by the morning sun, I stirred and got to my knees.

'There was the gate. There was the stile. I had dropped from exhaustion and terror right in front of them. Or had I been there all the time, and only imagined my fright of the night before? But no – there were my bruises and cuts. There were my shoes, back along the edge of the path where I'd run right out of them. It were real.

'Real? Well – it was as real as this table and this cup. It was real as yourself, Squire, for all the doubt in your eyes. You may think me a fool, but don't you judge me until you've been Piskie-led yourself, sir.'

I said nothing. I had been quite captivated by his tale, which had a character about it quite different from his usual story. It had a feeling of reality – or – at least a feeling that he himself truly believed it real.

He recovered himself, wiped his brow, and looked about expectantly, with the old craft and cunning in his eye, as the Lady of the House, who had been busying herself with domestic duties as John went on, took a seed-cake from the oven. His crest soon fell, however, as she set it in front of me, with a lump of fresh butter.

'You'll be wanting, Mr. Kneebone, I'm sure, to be getting on your way now, so as not to be late. You can wash your cup in the bowl, there, and good day to 'ee.' The good Mistress sent him on his way peremptorily.

As John shambled, disappointed, to the door, a young boy popped his head up in the corner where he had been lying and listening.

"'Oi! I thought you said you was goin' to tell us how you lost yer leg!"

Kneebone rounded on him as if to roar, but seeing me, he instead broke into a grin and said to the lad:

'Bless 'ee – I forgot entirely. Well – that's a story for another day.'

So there is why I have included this tale among all of the others. It was the first tale I ever heard from him that, however fantastic, might be true, and, for the first time, he forgot to mention his leg, and the whole enterprise failed miserably!

I soon made short work (well – the boy and I) of the cake and, having finished my tea, I thanked my hostess (with a small coin) and collected my horse (and parted with another small coin) and went on my way.

I said at the beginning that I have had no truck with superstition. But I wonder. We Christians have been on this island only a short time. We have spent much of it fighting with each other for and against some detail of worship, about who is in authority, and over words and language in the services. Much blood has been spilt over matters relating to the Prince of Peace.

I have never yet heard of a single drop of blood wasted over matters pertaining to the Old Gods, except when their believers are persecuted by we Christians. I have overheard many prayers for health, a child, a good harvest and many other desires being made in Church, and seldom have I seen a material manifestation of any sort of satisfaction of those prayers.

Yet I have seen swelling bellies on wives who, after years of barrenness, have visited the Wise Woman of their village and drunk potions, inhaled vapours, and had visions of gods and spirits whom they supplicated and entreated to send them a child.

So what it the 'right' of it? I'm not the one to ask. As I said, I'm a good Churchman, to whom such pagan things must not signify.

With My Name On It

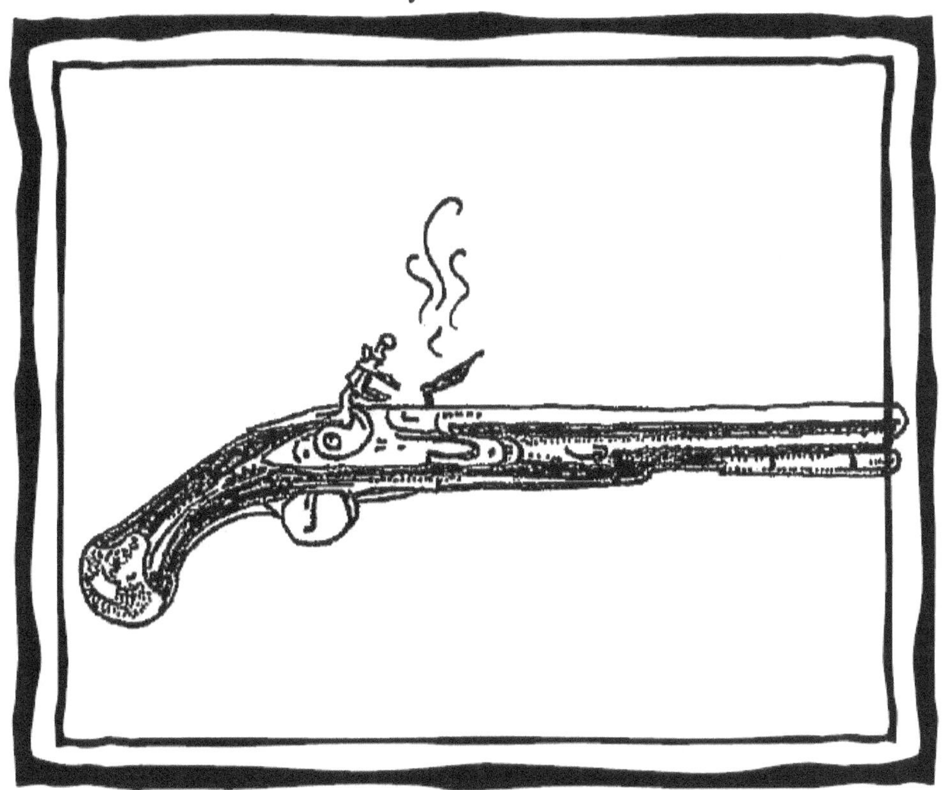

Sailors and the Sea come up often in these tales, as you will have noticed. Cornwall is a great place for men of the sea, from fishermen to world-travelers. Cornwall is surrounded on almost all sides by salt water, and cut off from England almost entirely by fresh, the river Tamar. It's only a little strip of land that allows one to walk into Cornwall without getting one's feet wet.

There is also a Cornish language, as features in the tale that now comes to mind. It's often called 'Old Cornish,' and has much in common with

Welsh and Breton. I expect that a scholar could tell you how they all started from one language, way backalong, but I'm no scholar, I fear.

Incidentally, I am just now reminded of a little story – a sort of joke, I suppose. I have told it before to surprise people with the knowledge that they actually know two words of the old Cornish tongue.

On the great ships of adventure and exploration many of the seamen are Cornishmen. It was on the sea, on ships and fishing boats, that many speakers of Old Cornish held on to their beloved language, after our English – friends – exerted enough influence on our Cornish ways to make the language almost extinct in the current day.

In any case (I do ramble, don't I?) on those great ships and their years-long journeys to far off places the crew were often Cornish and the officers, scientists, chaplains and other such Gentlemanly sorts were mostly English. One day in the far southern oceans – from which word has started to come of a vast, frozen continent – as there was nothing much to see above decks – there being only some insignificant, uninhabited islands nearby, the officers and such kept warm in their quarters while the Cornish sailors froze above. Pity the poor watchman in the crow's-nest in the sleet and hail!

At length, one of the Naturalists came up on deck for a smoke and noticed an odd-looking bird scuttling over the rocks and into the sea on a nearby island. He remarked to a nearby sailor on how comical it looked and said 'Well – I suppose we'd better think of a name for it, hadn't we?'

The sailor answered back "Ee's got a name, yer Honour. We gave it 'en.'

Naturally, the English gentleman was surprised and amused that these rustic Cornishmen would dare to impose on the right of their betters to name new species and such, but the Naturalist was a tolerant sort.

'And what name, pray tell, have you invented for that bird?' He asked. 'Well – 'ere comes another. Look you, my robin – take the glass, now – mark his head. What colour do you call that 'ed now?'

'Well – mostly white, I suppose.'

'An' so it be. White as china clay. So we have called it a name in Old Cornish what means "White Head." That is, in our talk, "Pen Gwynn." '

The Naturalist was so tickled by this bit of impertinence that he entered it just that way in his log. Of course, he could only guess at the spelling, which gave us 'Penguin.' So you see – you know two words of Old Cornish.

But to the tale. Young men have always, I've found, been rather susceptible to Kneebone's fables. Why, I'm sure I don't know, but it may have something to do with the setting of the stories, at least when told to young sailors, soldiers, miners and such in a way that encourages dreams of glory, titillates with hints of vice and sin and winks at petty cowardice and personal failing. Most young men would respond, I suppose, to such an appeal, especially if the young man were embarking on a career which might involve conflict, exotic locales and danger.

It was to just such a young man (a sailor, home on leave before his first great voyage) that Kneebone told such a tale. The young Tar had had the poor judgment to ask Kneebone how he became one-legged. As so many poor souls do, bless them.

'Well,' said Kneebone 'Get me a pint and I will tell you.' And the unsuspecting sailor signaled the tavern keeper for two more pints, which were duly drawn and brought to the pair. Kneebone took a deep draught, and the only sound was his clunking and the crackling of the fire as everyone in the tavern strained to hear his story.

'I grew up in this town' started John mournfully, 'They call it Penzance now, but it used to be known as Buriton back along; the town around the castle, though no one alive could tell you where that castle was. It's a hard life here – even the mayor kept his job more with force and violence! John Carveth that were, and he was a mean one, I tell you! He married well and thought that marrying the widow of the mayor made him mayor material. He fell out with near everyone, and so when it came time to elect the new mayor, he knew they would not elect him, so he prevented the election and just acted as though he were mayor, and so did his opponent Mr Tonkin, too. Its only when he went up against Bishop Trelawney that he was finally beaten. Terrible it was with his carrying on. Anyway, I was young when all that happened, but I saw it all. When I were eleven I had to choose between the Navy or working in the Wherry mine.'

'Why didn't you pick the mine?' said the listening sailor, slightly bitterly.

'Have you seen en?' Said John 'The sea goes in en twice a day - the main shaft do open between low and high tide! Imagine working seventeen fathoms under the sea, with the sea roaring and complaining above you, hell burning beneath you and the roof always leaking and letting the sea in on you, that's when the tide id'n running down the shaft. Then the work is hard, backbreaking t'is. Hot, dirty, heavy and dangerous – you're being broiled alive as you struggle to break and shift the ore. Oh there's tin there, and cobalt too, but honest, I tell you, it's a short life working the sea mines. No wonder the tinners rioted – they called up the militia and everything when all they there tinners all rioted on the Mount. No; I do stay at grass I do. So I picked the sea instead, thinking it were easier but we had a right old time of it.

'I were on a refitted ship, The Superb, one time. Our cousins in Little Britain had made it and sailed it out of Lorient, and then the navy caught if off the lizard. Now the Navy call it a French ship caught by the English, but I call it a Breton ship on loan from our cousins, 'tis. We have more in common with they in Brittany than they do with France, or we do with England, and don't let none tell you different. Their fishermen would come right into the bay here and we do used to talk to they in Old Cornish, and they would reply in their own language, and we would understand each other. Anyway, the navy refitted it, and we sailed it. We were sent off to America to Porto Bello. We were at war with Spain, as I have heard we are at war again. 'Course, they haven't tried to land here again, like they did before when they burned the place.

'Twenty ships there was, all told. All under the command of the right Rear-Admiral Francis Hosier, for the purpose of blocking up the Spanish galleons or seizing them should they venture out of the port. We arrived in June, back in '28 t'was, or maybe '26. Anyway, we didn't even try to take Porto Bello; just inspected every ship that went in or out.

Apparently, those were our orders, or so I heard tell. Well, they just unloaded their valuables and waited, didn't they? We never fired a single shot, and neither did they. They didn't need to, neither; American plague it was, and it ran round all the crews. Have you seen men dying by the thousands? It started with fever and muscle pain, but them that weren't throwing up, or eyes red and raw were dying with red faces or tongues. Most of our boys died, terrible, terrible I tell you. I spent as long as I could in the crow's nest, so I wouldn' have to look at everyone dying. But I could still hear the screams and cries. I could smell them too. I never caught it, me, but then some few didn't, sure enough.

'Anyway, things got so bad that Hosier had to leave for Jamaica and round up more crew and supplies and that's when they sent out a whole fleet of treasure ships from Porto Bello heading all the way to Spain. A whole fleet! And we missed them. By the time we got back, they were long gone; slipped through the remaining blockade and them that weren't dead. Hosier was hopping mad at that, and then he died, of course. He wad'n chucked over the side like the sailors, oh no. His body was wrapped in a proper sheet and put in the hold of his ship. Then his replacement died too. I think his replacement too died. Or did he survive? No, wait, that's it; Hosier's replacement was himself replaced in Jamaica, and then got to be replacement again, yes, when Hopson died. So it went Hosier, St Lo, Hopson, St Lo. We were calling him the coffin admiral, as he kept filling plague shoes. Until he died too, that is. It were hopeless, those three years in hell. It's just as well the war ended, or we would still be waiting there, not firing a shot, as they sat there tight in their port waiting for us all to die.

'And you lost your leg there?' said the sailor, impressed. John Kneebone looked a bit shifty.

'Well, not there as such, no' he said, 'See when we were there, right at the start, we caught several of their treasure ships. When everyone was dying they still kept tight watch over them, like a mother hen do watch over her chicks. But people were dying and things got a bit confused, and by the time we got back 'ere, there was no treasure to be had. Young Edward Boscawen, he were on the Superb – the same ship as me - and he thought maybe Hosier on the Breda had taken it for himself. Well, him being the son of a toff, they all believed him. Hosier took a lot of the blame of that trip. It's just as well he's dead, still *Neb na gare y gwayn coll restoua - He that heeds not gain, must expect loss.*

'Ten years passed and a new customs gentleman, right here in town, Nicholas Teage his name was, well he somehow got it in his head that I might know a thing or two about where the gold had gone to. He ran me up and down the town; run me ragged he did. Things get a bit crazy around St John's eve. They hold bonfires all over Cornwall that night, but Penzance goes one better. They put tar barrels up on poles around the quay and light them and hold processions with torches and fireworks and everything. 'Tis a magnificent sight! They dance the eye of the needle dance too. In all that, Teage was looking for a sailor in a town full of them. He caught sight of me by the light of the tar barrels, right on the quay, and chased me up quay street, and up chapel street. I thought I would give him the slip in one of the taverns on chapel street and I ducked into one of them. Teage finally entered, and saw my distinctive coat, and shouted. Everybody ran, but he stayed on his quarry, and he followed out the back.

'Did Teage stab you in the leg?' asked the sailor, eagerly. John looked injured

'Not as such, no, not as such' John said 'he did stab the man, and I'm sorry about that, because I had given him my coat knowing Teage would follow him and not me. I've heard tell since that the landlord found Teage in his back yard looking wild eyed and shocked in the flickering lights. He looked like a man come from the gump and seen the revels there. He couldn't believe that he, a government officer, had killed someone accidentally, without meaning to. The landlord saw his predicament, and he led Teage inside, and he and a couple of shoremen buried the man right there in the pub without a word to no one. So I heard tell, anyway. There are some unkind souls who call the landlord a greedy man who noticed how one of his guests seemed to have rather a lot of money and he used Teage's well known pursuit of myself as cover in order to kill his guest and steal his money, and put about quietly that Teage had done it accidentally, but I do know that I never saw that fancy coat again.

'No; what happened was, when he started hunting me, all the smugglers and pirates in the town started thinking that maybe he had a point. One of the worst was Richard Green; oh he would give Mr. Carveth a run for his money now, all the robbery and violence he could do. It were he what caught me, that same night right after I had given my coat to that stranger. I turned around and there he was smiling at me, like you would at a prize cow. He caught me and took me to his house. He started off fairly polite, but after a couple of days it became clear he was not going to let me go without me giving him the location to the Spanish treasure. He locked me in a shed in his yard. He thought I would give him anything but *Gwell yw gwetha vel goofen*, — It is better to keep than beg.

'A week after St John's eve he ran out of patience. He thought if he sliced off my toes, I would tell him where the treasure was to, but I didn't. So after another week he thought if he cut off my foot, I would tell him then, and I didn't. Then he thought I might give in if he cut off my shin. He did that the following week. He had it all planned out. He was taking his time, cutting me up a bit at a time. He used a butcher's knife to slice through my bone, and poured boiling pitch on the wound to keep me alive. Or dead; I'm never too sure on that. If I didn't talk when he cut off my left knee, I still had my left thigh. He planned to carry on with my right leg, then my fingers and treat my arms in the same way, until I told him where the treasure was, or died. I think, though, that someone maybe heard some of my screams, or maybe someone had seen Richard Green take me to his home on St John's Eve, or maybe fate was finally helping me out.

'It was I was lying, bloody, on his table, right after he poured hot pitch on my leg where he had cut off my left thigh below the hip when in burst none other than Nicholas Teage! He attacked Richard straight off and they tipped the table over and me with it. I was in agony, but I crawled out of that hell hole as they fought over me, as quickly as I could. Outside I found I could barely stand, but I think I could have given a two-legged man a run for speed that night as I hopped out of his yard. I heard a gun go off as I hid in a nearby cellar. Well, killing another sailor is one thing, but to kill a customs officer is something else. Mr. Green had to depart sudden for sunnier climes. I believe he is now somewhere in the Indian Ocean, plying his vicious trade.

'I have had time to heal now. I need to return to Jamaica, I tell you.'

'So you DID hide the treasure?' asked the sailor, his eyes gleaming.

'Not as such, no, not as such' said John 'Its just that I believe young Edward Boscawen is a captain there now; I just want to find him and maybe ask him to tell me where he hid it all. Perhaps in one of those forts they levelled, he with his buddy Sir Charles Knowles.

With that, John Kneebone got up to relieve himself, shuffling off leaning on his crutch. The landlord came over with two more jugs and the sailor paid him. A heavyset man got up from the next table and approached him. The stranger leaned in conspiratorially and whispered 'I hope he is giving you good value for your ale.'

'What do you mean?' asked the sailor, suspiciously.

'Well, he tells a good tale, when he can remember, but what I heard was that he lost that leg at Wheal Malkin, when his explosive caused a roof fall that crushed it. Took six men to dig him out, I heard, and his leg was done for and they had to take it off. Then the nearest he's been to sea is that Pentreath woman; the fishwife from Mousehole who gives him those phrases in the Old Cornish that he's using on you. Him with a wife and cheeld vean in Sithney, too! As for Richard Green, he may or may not be a vicious smuggler, and he may or may not have killed Mr Teage, but what I have heard is that he and Kneebone were as thick as thieves for many a year – like brothers they were. He's spinning you a good yarn, I hope the ale is worth it.' And with that the stranger left.

Soon Kneebone reappeared and resumed his seat. He moved to raise his jug when the sailor's hand pressed it gently but firmly down and he said 'I've just heard that you made all that up; that your leg was lost in a mining accident and the most you know about the sea is what a fishwife from Mousehole gives you.'

'Well, *nyn ges goon heb lagas, na kei heb scovarn,* — There is no downs without eye, no hedge without ears' sniffed John, and just as firmly removed the sailor's hand and raised his jug to his lips 'I'll admit what I told you was not the whole gospel truth. Some troublemakers have been around recently, stirring people up. Wesley I believe one was called. Came by last year 'twas with their fire and brimstone; got people sneaking on each other everywhere. These new Wesleyans like to spread what they will and hate the Old Cornish too. They are not having it all their own way here, though, and while folk will listen to them, they do like to keep the old ways too.

'We agreed to change the story, me and Richard, to protect...' John paused, 'Anyway he's gone so there is no one for me to care about protecting, now, so I will tell you the gospel truth. Richard Green is a good man, sure enough, and I would call him a friend if I could ever find him. The clues were there. Why did ten years pass after I came home before Teage started chasing me? He replaced the useless Henry Badcock back in 1734. Yes, all that time I was in Sithney, where I worked and raised a family. I was visiting my friend, Richard Green, when his mother, the oh-so saintly Anne Green; long suffering widow of this parish, she started telling people that I had taken the treasure ships and hidden the treasure years before. It was she who didn't like me standing her son a round in the pub, who saw my fancy clothes bought from the honest sweat of my brow and added two and two together to make six. It was she who started tongues wagging and set Nicholas Teage on his ill-fated journey.

'But she didn't stop at being a gossip. When Richard hid me in his home while Teage tore up Penzance looking for me, she went to Teage and told him that I was holding her son hostage! When Teage burst through the door that night, he was holding two guns. Me and Richard jumped at him. The first shot would have killed me had Richard not smacked his arm down. As it is, Teage still shot me in the leg, and in the following struggle he took the second shot from his other gun. The gun I had turned on him. Richard told people he killed Teage to stop his dear, sweet old mother from telling people I had killed the customs man. He got me to a friendly surgeon that night; a miner's surgeon who took off my damaged leg. Then he disappeared, and I haven't seen him since then.

Just then the landlord offered round some roasted woodcocks he had bought at the market that day. The sailor stood John a meal for his tale and they ate in companionable silence. With John's tale over, the murmur of talk resumed, and the landlord chucked a couple more logs on the fire. It began to rain, and hammered on the small window behind them, but for now they were snug in the warmth of the fire.

Finally the sailor finished, and called for more ale for himself and John. 'What will you do now?' he asked.

'I know you don't believe a word I've said,' murmured Kneebone 'But I would dearly like to know what Captain Boscawen did with all that Spanish gold. That lad will go far, sure enough, but I'd like to knaw that there's a small bit of treasure out there somewhere, with my name on it.'

John Kneebone's Tale

I include this next tale with some trepidation, as it seems to contain me. Please be assured that the following is just as much an invention of John Kneebone's as the rest.

I had known a young man when I was myself a stripling, he being the son – the second son – of a fine house in – well – let's not go into detail, but suffice it to say that it was in England, and that any Englishman would know the name of the house and the family.

As second son, he, thanks to primogeniture, found that he had much time to fill. As a young lad, he had loved to draw, and his talent was noticed by his doting parents. They encouraged him to study art, sending him to Paris to learn from the famous painters there.

He wasn't one to become the next Leonardo, I fear, but his talent and skill developed to the point that his works were to be found in the best galleries in London, and on the walls of Manor houses the length and breadth of the land. His favourite subject, dear ob'm (as we Cornish folks say), was the coast of Cornwall in all its wild and tumultuous varieties.

One day, years after he had established himself as a Master of his art, I met him at an Inn in a coastal town, where he was staying while seeking out suitable and as yet unpainted (by him) Cornish locales worthy of his brush. We had a pleasant time together, reminiscing and talking of old friends. I can only guess that, at some point in that visit, perhaps during a walk that we took down by the quayside, we had been seen together by John Kneebone. What else would have possessed Kneebone to include me in this tale, I can't imagine.

I heard the tale, of course, from my friend as he was finishing his Cornish sojourn. With several canvases filled, and with a brimming sketch-book against further creations, he supped with me on the eve of his parting, and said, as we relaxed with a post-prandial pipe and glass,

'Here's an extraordinary thing, old man. As I sat at my easel on the clifftop, there came along as ragged a creature as I've ever beheld. Fine ruined face, missing a leg and with a bizarre tale to tell, in which he included you! As I wanted to get a sketch of him, I gave him ear. You really must hear this, you know. It was so riveting, once started, that I can hear every word now as if he were speaking in my ear as we sit here. To get him talking, and staying, I asked him how he came to lose his leg. Here's what he said…'

'Gammy I was called, sir. Gammy Kneebone. Some as can be very cruel when they've a mind… All very well you askin' now how I came by that name, an' 'ow this 'ere awful misfortune befell me – but seein' as 'ow you asked so nice, I'll tell 'ee.

'I'm seein' you're a h'artist now – an' very nice too. Well, I 'ave a bit of talent in that direction meself… there was some as tole me I should send me paintings up to London, they was so fine. Fine eye for detail I 'ave y'see… but o' course, what with workin' all hours God made at the fishin' an' suchlike, never had the free time that a gentleman such as yerself might have to play with such things. But I kept at 'en, an' though I say so as shudden, my pitchers was acclaimed by all an' sundry near an' far.

'Well – this ere leg, well, this leg that <u>ain't</u> 'ere, maybe I should say… 'ow it came about was like this see. I was down Mouzel, working at the fishin', an' t'was all me an' the missus could do to keep the clothes on our backs, I tell 'ee. Five childern we 'ad too, mind – an' all young'uns, all bleatin' an' mitherin' all day, an' she out doing the laundry for the lord an' lady as well to make ends meet. Meet, did I say? Dammee, we was lucky if the ends come within sight of each other… 'tis no lie to say we was struggling good an' proper. You bein' a fam'ly man like meself, I'm certain you'll knaw the way of it. They d'bring their love, folks say – but dammee, they d'keep 'ee poor too.

'But still, I 'ad me paintin'… well, tis some conceit, I'm sure you'll say, to think I may earn a crust from such a pastime. But 'ope, see – 'ope is a wondrous thing… an' maybe the good Lord would look with favour upon my poor efforts, who's to say?

'I spent all me spare time climbing out along they cliffs there looking for h'elegant sights for me paintin'… an' I 'ad this one place that took me just right. 'Ansum, it was – just other side of the 'arbour there, up past Mousehole cave, out towards the Kemyels at Point Spaniard… a view as a man would dream of. A sight to make the heart sore with longin'… I bethought meself that I could render this into a vision t'would make a man's 'eart bleed for want of 'is 'omeland. An' there, see – tha's the thing… take a man away from 'is 'omeland, an' 'e d'grieve, see… an 'if that 'omeland is Cornwall, well, now – that grieving is like a canker, a sore, that waint be 'ealed till 'e's back 'ome again.

'So this 'ere was the nub of me plan see – to make a paintin' so filled with God's beauty on this Cornish earth, that nawthen would serve the poor Cornishman exiled away from 'is country but that he must buy it an' 'ang it on 'is wall straightway, to give 'is 'eart ease, as it were… mind you, when I say "poor", I mean truly, the "rich" Cornishman, for t'was my intention to charge a pretty penny for my work on this 'ere creation – for after all, was not me own heart an' soul in every stroke of that brush an' in every dab of that paint?

'So there was I, up 'pon the cliff, me easel an' paints before me, an' me eyes on that vision – days, weeks indeed – creatin' me wondrous creation. Some days, if the weather was kind, the dear childern would come along there with me to gaze upon that sight, an' to play among the heather an' the furzy, an' make camps in the boulders. Then maybe we'd 'ave a bit o' picnic up there – a proper fayst, indeed… bit o' saffern cake or a corner o' pasty… My littlest one, the baby Marsha – well, I say baby, she were going on 'bout 3 year old then, bless 'er – she took a fancy to this paintin lark 'erself, an' I giv'd 'er a little board of 'er own an' 'er own brush, an' she'd sit beside me, 'appy as a clam, daubin' away… would'n call King George 'er uncle…

'Well, all was going along just fine an' dandy… then one day, somethin' happened as put all in a fine pickle. The wife, working away at the washin' for him an' she up at the big house, never gave no mind to 'ow the young'uns was goin on… My eldest, Mary-Jane, was left in charge, an' dammee if the littlest one didn't get away from 'er big sister an' straight out the door, slippery as an eel… an' Mary-Jane, well, she didn't know what to do for the best… she 'ad the three other little ones there too, mind.

'So she 'ammered on next door an' called up Granny Pezzick… now, Granny Pezzick is a bit deef, but she come round straight away, an' Mary-Jane left Granny Pezzick to mind the littl'uns, an' off she traipsed, uplong an' outlong, downlong an' inlong, looking for that dear child. Well – t'was no matter where she looked, she cudden see sight nor sign…

'Well poor Mary-Jane was in some state, I tell'ee… then who should come along but that theer John Wearne. You must know of un… very well-respected man in these ere parts, an' I should say a very great chum o' mine. Me an' John go way back, y'see – an' folks'll tell ee, we're thick as thieves, as it were... 'Ee d'look out for me, see, an' me fer 'im… Any'ow… along come John, an' seein' my maid in such a tear, he up an' ast' 'er fer the cause of 'er distress… Well, she lost no time in telling of 'im, you can be sure, 'ow as my little Marsha 'ad up an' off like that, an' who was to say where to she was gone to now. Well, the tellin' of the awful tale upset Mary-Jane all over again, an' she weepin' an' wailin', feared 'er life what 'er mammy was goin' t'say when she come 'ome.

'Well, didn't take John long to apprise 'isself of the particklers of the situation, an' 'e soon 'stablished that Mary-Jane 'ad done a fair job in searchin' out all of Mouzel looking for the dear lost child. "Now look 'ere, Mary-Jane," says John, all business-like, for to calm 'er nerves somewhat an' leave 'er know 'e 'ad the matter in 'and… "Is there anywhere else 'round 'ere where Marsha d'belong to go from time to time, somewhere she might fancy to go lookin' for?"

"Well, sir," says Mary-Jane, dryin' 'er eyes with 'er anky (which she d'always carry up 'er knicker-leg, as 'er mammy taught 'er – she's a good girl, my Mary-Jane)… "Well, sir, she d'go down harbour beach sometime, but I bin there already sir! An over behind the quay, but she idden there neither!"

"Well, come on now, think a bit 'arder, Mary-Jane… where else?" says John now, sounding a bit stern…

"Well she've been up over the cliff, past Raginnis, where Fayther d'go sometimes with 'is paints… she d'seem to like it out that way… I abben bin out there yet, sir… only I'm a bit chary goin' up there on my own, like, as Fayther do get in some tight spots up there to do 'is bit o' paintin' sir, an' I d'get worrit…"

"Right, well, <u>now</u> I see the way of it," says John… "Now don't you worry none Mary-Jane, you an' me shall go together to see if your Marsha 'ave gone a-wanderin' up there lookin' for 'er Da…" So, all was settled, an' John an' Mary-Jane set off up Raginnis, she lookin' under every bush an' callin' out all the way as they was proceedin' along… "Marsha? Marsha? Where are 'ee my ansum? You come to Mary-Jane now, you 'ear?"

'Well they saw nor 'eard nawthen, an' soon came out atop the cliff, over Mouzel cave. Still no sign of my Marsha – so on they come, an' twad'n long before they sighted me sat there 'mongst they git rocks a-paintin' – absorbed, as it were, gripp't by the muse, an' with no notion of the drama that was h'unfoldin' around me. Suddenly I 'ears this call – "John! John!! Is that you there, boy? This 'ere's John Wearne… I got your Mary-Jane with me.." Well, took me up short, I c'n tell 'ee… I wadden' expectin' no visitors like…

'Well soon they come up over the cliff, an' I could see Mary-Jane was in some state… an' John an' she lost no time in puttin' it all afore me in all its horrid detail… that our Marsha was missin' an' would not be discovered, come what may. Well, then all three of us took to 'ollerin' an' callin' around, an' suddenly John 'eared somethin'… "Hush!! Hush, boy!" he cried – an' we all fell silent an' strained our ears, an' sure nuff, I 'eared un too… twas my little maid, callin' fer 'er da… but where she were to, I cudden truly say. "Da! Da!" She was crying, an' I callin' back to 'er, "Marsha, my flower! Where are 'ee to, my little maid?" But then I saw 'er, an' my 'and flew to my mouth…

'Well t'was a desperate situation, I'm tellin' of 'ee, an' Mary-Jane was as white as a sheet – an' I aren't shamed to say my 'eart was in my mouth too… for there was Marsha, perched on a rock below us all, half-way up the cliff, tryin' to climb up to 'er da… but she was on the edge of a damn git zawn there an' could get no further, an' the sea boilin' beneath 'er… well, I can't think of it now but I d'feel sick with the fright of it.

Well, John, bless 'is soul, 'ee offered to run back to Mouzel an' fetch a rope to climb down to the little maid an' bring 'er safely away from 'arm – an' 'ee didden falter, but up an' off fast as he could go. Well, Mary-Jane an' me was in some pother, as to what to do fer the best – an' in the end I could stand it no longer, but I must climb down meself an' try an' save 'er.

'Then Mary-Jane got this notion to break up me easel, an' to use the struts to try an' reach across to Marsha, an' with my approval she set about it with a will. Well, you will understand sir, there was nawthen further from me mind at that point but the state of my paintin 'pon the easel – for who could think of such fripperies with the life of my little Marsha there 'anging in the balance? So I set off, clamberin' over the git boulders an' squeezin' between they narra gaps, edgin' closer an' closer to my little maid, with that there stick in me 'and. Well, course, she's started cryin' now an' was lookin' as if she would take it into 'er 'ead to jump towards me – which would a'bin the ending of us both, I'm sure.

'Last I managed to get close enough for 'er to grab fast the stick… "Hold tight to this 'ere stick Marsha, now – you be a good girl for yer da, an' hold on tight. Don't let go, mind!!" I called to her, an' she stopped crying an' sat down, holding the end of the stick so tight, like it was my 'and itself, and me 'oldin' tight to t'other end… Well, it took all my strength, but I managed to 'ang on to the rocks an' drag myself round to where she was – but just as I reached 'er, a stone give way beneath me foot an' nex' thing, me leg 'as disappeared down a 'ole, an' I'm stuck fast. Well I made a grab for Marsha, an' praise the lord, I caught 'er just as she was about to plummet to 'er certain death in the icy waters below. I 'eld 'er tight to me as I could – thanking the Lord for 'is mercy – an' set about ponderin' on how I might best get she an' me out of this pickle we were in, <u>and</u> in good 'ealth.

'Well, Mary-Jane was above us, wringing 'er hands, an' calling down to me, "Da! Da!! Is Marsha all right?? Wa's 'appenin' da? Can you bring 'er back up safely? Oh mercy, Da, what are we to do?!!"

Well, who should turn up then but that most faithful of all fellows, John Wearne, an' carryin' a stout rope, an' with him some half dozen fine fellows from the 'arbour, all eager to effect a rescue of me an' little Marsha. So John throws down the rope – well, not <u>all</u> the rope, you follow, but one end of it – an' somehow I manages to tie it tight around Marsha's waist an' shoulders – she crying at me all the while, for she was 'appy nuff just to stay cuddlin' in 'er da's arms. "Well, John Wearne – 'aul away now, if you will', I called up… 'but 'ave a care, mind – tha's my 'eart an' soul on the end of that there rope!"

'So little Marsha was drawn away from me up through the air, an' I watched with great fear an' trepidation that something awful might 'appen to 'er on 'er perilous journey – might she crash against they rocks, or the rope fer to slip, or – calamity! – snap, or come undone, an' my little maid be dashed an' lost forever! But no, all was well, an' she soon was safely received by willin' 'ands reachin' out to 'er, an' pulled to safety.

'Well – in some respects I could now breathe easy – if it weren't for the fearful pain that now gripped me nether regions…I was truly caught fast, an' the more I squirmed an' wriggled an' pushed an' pulled to try an' h'extricate myself from this quandary, the more firmly gripped I became, an' the more stone an' dirt went down to jam the hole. I made sure that John, with Marsha an' my Mary-Jane (who was beside 'erself with worry about me – but there was nought she could do fer me, of course, dear child), would set off now back to Mouzel an' deliver my childern back to their rightful 'ome – where, with good fortune, their mammy would likely even now be pacin' the floor with worry for their safe return. She was expected back by now, an' would 'ave 'eard the dretful tale from Granny Pezzick, I was sure.

'Well – still there were some saviours above me, plottin' 'ow to retrieve me in one piece from my awful predicament… so one tied 'issell to the rope (John Wearne 'avin' left it there for just such a purpose), the others 'oldin' fast to t'other end, an' proceeded to climb down as best 'e could towards me. After some palaver, 'ee got near nuff to see that I was in some coddle… one leg was invisible, swallowed up by the native rocks of Cornwall, an' the other caught up above ground, but all of me, caught like a rat in a trap, an' no moving of me for love nor money. My rescuer freed 'issself from the rope an' sent it back for a second man to join us – but when' e' come down, e' could see there was nawthen to be done. They 'ad a go at pullin me up like a cork out a bottle, but the only result was me yellin' fit to bust, an' I moved not an inch. One bright spark 'ad an idea, an' sent down to the cove for some fish oil – an' in due course that arrived, was passed down to me by rope, an' poured all round my leg in that 'ole, with a view to easin' the passage of the trapped limb – but t'was all in vain. All th'oil did was to turn the fallen stone an' dirt into a paste that set as hard as the rock itself, an' gripped me leg all the tighter.

'Well, the day was drawin' on, an' t'would soon be dark. My saviours could see no way forward nor back. Last, the fateful decision was made. There was only one way to save me from the freezin' waters, rising fast below me, an' bein' left to the mercy of the h'elements as night approached. I must go, an' leave my leg behind me.

'Well – t'was not a plan I 'ad much likin' for, sir, if I'm to be honest with 'ee – but I could see no other way. Better for me to go back to me family deficient by one leg, an' for my Marsha to be saved an' to grow up the fine young woman she is today – than – well, the other notion, don't bear thinkin' about.

'So one o' they young men went back down to the cove for a saw, an' a bottle o' brandy… an' me 'avin' drained the bottle dry to numb the pain, the deed was done. The surgeon was there waitin' for me as I was brung up – well, the pain, I can't tell 'ee sir. T'was dretful, just dretful… brandy ur no brandy. So I was stitched up – to spend the rest o' my days shamblin' around with a peg leg an' a stick, an' bein' called Gammy Kneebone. An' there's many have made light of that surname too, sir, as you may imagine. I 'ave become a figure of fun to some 'ereabouts. But I s'pose 'tis some consolation to think that the 'Kneebone' of old Gammy will be part of they Cornish cliffs now and forever more!

'And now – well, I'll be truthful with you sir – life is 'ard. Since the loss of the leg, ere, I idden much use on the boats no more – an' after me easel was broke up, an' me paintin', that I'd pinned all me 'opes on for all they weeks, that was goin' to be the savin' of my family – trampled in the dirt by those savin' of me life – well, there's not much to complain about, if your life is bein' saved, is there, sir? An' since that dretful day, the 'eart 'ad gone out of me for the paintin' – I was thinkin' I would'n be liftin' a brush no more…

'But I'm 'ere now, sir – an' I'm lookin' at this god-given gift you 'ave for makin' your pictures so fine, an' I can feel the old fire burnin' up in me veins again – seeing that paint spreading across me board, kindlin' the feelin' I could make somethin' <u>ansum</u>, that some folks might want to pay money for… to make meself useful to me family again, an' not such a burden as I 'ave become. Well, with the fishin' gone, an' me so clumsy, like, on getting' around, there idden much I can turn me 'and to, really – but I could paint, sir. I <u>could</u> do that. I'd 'ave another go at the paintin' – if I <u>could</u>. But tis all a dream tha's been taken from me sir… for where would a poor cripple like me find the wherewithal to set meself up again with the paintin', eh, sir? But I don't complain, mind! You won't 'ear a word of complaint pass my lips! I thank the lord every day for the saving of my maid Marsha – an' wa's one leg gone? Dammee – I've got another, abben I?

'An' the paintin… why, tis only the fancy of old Gammy Kneebone, sir…

'And well – I hope my tale abben been a tedious one for you, sir… but you did ask…'

I didn't ask my friend if he had paid Kneebone for his time and his tale, but I have no doubt that John's pocket was a bit heavier as he left the clifftop. For myself, I consider myself well-paid for having been dragooned into one of John's tales simply by being honoured as fodder for his imagination. How many of us, after all, can be both living soul and fictional character at once? Not many, I'm sure, and it rather tickles my fancy that I am so!

The Brewer's Tale
(An Anonymous Gentleman Speaks)

Squire Wearne has asked me to write this account. He gives me credit for being a man of some intelligence – although whether you will agree with him when you have heard my tale, I can't say. This tale is held by Mr. Wearne to be of some special significance, as it contains the last time that John Kneebone was seen in Cornwall.

I do have some education, having been born into a family of some means – brewers, in fact, and of a popular ale. I learned my letters at home, and then was sent to school.

I have not always followed the lessons I learned at school. They taught us not to gamble, and I gambled. They taught us not to drink, and I drank. They taught us not to steal, and I stole. In fact, had my father not been who he was, I probably would have been hanged long ago.

I once came close to hanging. Not because of any particular crime that I had committed, although I was in gaol, but due to the machinations and dastardly betrayal by one who the Squire knows too well, John Kneebone.

As I said, I have stolen. Among other crimes. Why, since I was scion of a family who had much when many had nothing, who could provide my needs and wants, did I steal? I still struggle to understand the powerful forces inside me that urged me to do the illegal, the cruel, the hurtful.

As a small child, I first derived pleasure from hurting things. I would slap the dog to hear it whine and snarl. Mother or Cook or someone would always be close by to restrain it from attacking me. I made sure that someone was close by to see to that before I abused the animal. I chased and kicked at the geese in the yard, though I was too small to do them much damage.

As I grew, I took out my lust for cruelty by bullying smaller and weaker children. Always the smaller and weaker. You have already guessed that I am, among other things, a coward. I became adept at concealing my violence with an angelic countenance and protestations of innocence. Mother was inclined to dote on me.

I was, on leaving school, employed in the family business. I drove the drays which delivered the barrels of our beer to the pubs, and unloaded the barrels with great sweat and strain, which I hated and resented. The son of the Owner should not have to break his back and bruise his hands labouring like a common navvy. But I thought that this was my route to more gentle employment, and I put up with it.

I was eventually set to work learning the brewer's art. Those who quaff and guzzle ale have no idea how difficult and complicated it is to produce that product that they swill. One whiff of a wayward breeze through a cracked window or a badly-closed door will blow in wild yeast which will settle on the fermenting wort and spoil an entire run of beer, costing hundreds to the firm. A careless mishandling of a hose or a pipe, or the opening of the wrong valve will dump contaminants into the process and ruin a week's work.

Was I ever the cause of such an unclosed door, a fumbled hose, a misturned wheel? I have scars still that will answer that question to anyone who knew my father's temper or the cruelty of the foremen under whom I labored.

After a few years of work in the brewery, after I had grown into young manhood, I began to despair of ever being taken into the office to do soft-handed work like ordering grain and hops, totaling up accounts and invoicing the pubs. I felt doomed to toil forever in the stinking, gloomy, rancid brew-house.

I appealed to my mother. I told her a story I had concocted as I skimmed foam and scum from the fermenting wort, of an opportunity for great profit in a scheme put together by some friends. All lies, of course, but so much did she dote on me (she, too, feeling that what I was being forced by Father to do was beneath me) that she agreed to furnish me with funds – a few hundred – to invest and make my fortune.

I invested. Oh, how I invested. I invested in brandy, in whores, in cock-fights and horse-races, until the money was gone. Every penny. Obviously I could not go back as a Prodigal to my family. I had burned that bridge, and even my besotted mother now saw my true colours and turned her face from me.

All I had were my wits and my innate cunning, along with my cruelty. I had met many a ne'er-do-well and blackguard during my debauched spending and formed some of the worst of these (and the most easily cowed) into a gang. We turned to house-breaking, 'free-trading,' extortion and any number of criminal enterprises. We even had a junior gang of boys who would cut purses and raid the shops of unwary merchants and bring us the proceeds. We lived as we could in the caves along the coast, and never stayed in one place for long.

Naturally, such a life could not sustained forever. One of the gang was caught in a house-robbery and turned informant. One night as we sat around the fire, deep in a cave near Prussia Cove, a noise alerted us that the Law was closing in.

We scattered, running blindly in all directions. We had not been in that hide-out for long enough to have determined an efficient and effective getaway. I simply wanted to put distance between myself and the fire, to get out of the light and escape into the concealing darkness. In that fickle darkness, however, I found not concealment and succor, but betrayal. As I ran, my foot found nothing but air beneath it. I desperately tried to stop, but a moment later felt myself tumbling and falling. I knew no more for some time.

I awoke in horrible pain. I lay, as near as I could tell, on the rocks below the cave-mouth. It seemed, later when I could reflect on those terrible times, that when I fell, the tide had been in. The fall was not very far, and the water somewhat mitigated the impact of my body on what was below. There were rocks, of course, but, after I woke and lay on my back coughing brine from my throat, I saw that the tide had gone out. Thinking back, I must have lain there for several hours, for the tide to have gone out as far as it had. Air which had blown under my cloak as I fell must have formed a float of sorts which kept my unconscious head above water until the receding tide could lay me completely onto the rocks.

Water notwithstanding, the rocks had badly battered me. But it was not bruises which caused my agonizing condition. There was a wrecked fishing-boat tangled in the rocks beneath the cave mouth. I had almost missed it. Almost, except for my left leg. It had become wedged into the shards of the wreckage and had been cruelly pinched and twisted by the waves as I lay floating. When the tide lowered me to the rocks, my poor leg was still gripped by the wreck. The tightness of the entanglement kept the blood of my body from flowing out through the rents caused by the mangling wood, but the most of my leg, my left leg, was on the other side of that trap, and numb. I later learned that all of the blood had drained from it, leaving it a corpse's leg though the rest of me still lived.

I called out for help. The authorities had long since taken away those of my comrades that they could catch and were no doubt chasing the others through gorse and bramble. I was alone. I, of course, became fearful for my life. I called and called, hoping for some response other than the echoes from the cliff-walls. And the tide was turning.

My head was the first thing to feel the returning water. I tried, as well as I could, to move myself up toward the cliffs, but, with my poor leg still gripped in the wreck, I could manage no more than a couple of inches. I doubted if anything would float me this time, and dreaded the sea would slowly rise up the sides of my face, to cover my mouth and, soon after, my nose. Panic burned in me, but I was helpless.

A rattle of rocks. A voice.

'Oi! You there! Do you hear me!'

'Help me! Help me! I'm drowning!'

A confusion of sounds. Voices.

'Hold 'is head up, Johns. Get yer arms under his back, you two. Gentle, now, it may be broke. Jesus, will you look at that leg. Near sheared off from the hip down. Leamon! Wrap a turney-kit just where it comes out on this side to stop bleedin'. That leg's gone, but mebbe we can save the rest!'

My angels. Fishermen. Saw me from the path at the cliff-top on their way to their boat.

I had lost much blood and been through great shock. I must have fainted as they lifted me, though I no longer felt pain from my poor, almost-amputated leg. I woke in a doctor's surgery, though at the time I didn't know where.

At the foot of my bed stood a constable. Seeing me blink, he half-turned, keeping his eye on me the while (as if I were in any condition to try to escape) and called 'Captain!'

In came a familiar form. I had encountered Captain Sleeman often in my wild days.

'Well, lad – we've got you now good and propur. And it's sorry I am to have to arrest you in the condition you're in. I had hoped that you'd walk to the gallows one day, but now – well – you just look down here, why don't you.'

He pointed toward the foot of the bed, toward my left. Nothing. A familiar rise in the sheets showed that my right leg was where it had ought to be, but where a twin rise belonged on the left, nothing. A cold sweat jumped from my pores as I started a groan which turned into a shriek. The Captain stood there, staring, as I passed through the most horrifying seconds a man can pass through.

I made a slow recovery. In time, I was taken to Bodmin gaol to await trial. When the trial finally came, I found that my father had hired an advocate for me from the Capitol with the highest of reputations. It seemed that I had not forfeited all hope of parental pity. My mother looked pale and was weeping when they wheeled me, in a bath chair, into the courtroom.

As I hoped, the London man made fools of the local law-men. I wasn't to go scot-free, but was to be spared the noose and was given a sentence of a few months, back at Bodmin. I supposed that, as my family had decided to pity me, I might have a fairly comfortable time of it. Nice food and some comforts were not hard to come by in the gaol, if one could pay.

While serving my sentence, I was allowed to move about somewhat within the prison walls, as I was deemed, as a one-legged man, not to be likely to run away. Most days, I hobbled to a small yard which had a bit of grass and a tree to sit beneath and read.

One day, after a few weeks, I noticed that someone was already there. Annoyed, I rattled up with my crutch scraping noisily on the stones to order him away from my favourite spot and back to wherever he belonged. Then I stopped. For a moment, I thought that I must be suffering from a delirium. Here was a man, sitting on the ground, with my hair, my size, my color of eye, and, strangest of all, only one leg! His left leg, like mine, was missing from just below the hip.

We eyed each other.

'Well I'll be blowed,' He said, 'another yooneedexter.'

'I'm not sure, friend' Said I, 'What you mean by that, but if it's that I share your lack of leg, you have observed keenly. May I ask your name?'

'You first, mate.' He drawled as he ran his eye over me. 'Tellin' goes afore askin' in these sorts of negoosheatuns. How be you called, if I may be suffered to in-kwire?'

I told him my name without hesitation. It wasn't anything he couldn't find out for himself easily enough. I asked again for his name. 'Now here's a name you may have heard if you've lived in Wendron- or Helston, or Gweek, or Sithney or them en-viroons. Expeshully if y've been some on the rough and I guess that maybe you have. I'm called, like generations of my kin afore me, Kneebone. John Kneebone.'

I nearly guffawed at the idea of a one-legged man (though I was one myself) being called Kneebone, but a warning gleam in his eye suggested that I control myself.

'Mr. Kneebone…' I started.

'John will do for the likes of you, mate. You're hard up against it now, but I can tell by your talk that you've come to this from genteel beginnins. Jus' call me John and we'll be fast pals, as men of the road ought to be. Sit yourself – plenty of room for two – and we'll have a jaw – and a dram!'

He then pulled from under his shirt a small, leather bottle. He tugged off the cap, raised it to his lips, and took a healthy draught. He held it out to me and, sensing my hesitancy, waggled it and said 'Come on, friend. Any plague or pestilence I carry will be no match for what's in this 'ere jerrybowem. It's likelier to cure you then kill you.'

I accepted it and sipped and swallowed. A white fire seared my throat, but I was damned if I would cough in the light of his appraising eyes.

'That's right, lad.' He cackled. 'Well done. Most men wouldn't stand up to a swaller of the true potcheen of Ireland so well. It's an old, old mate I got this from. Eamon knows how to get the real aqua-veet, to be sure. Now we're good friends – and we are good friends ain't we, squire – we can have a good ole palaver to while away our time in durance vile.'

Nothing loath – as there was no secret to my story – I let him know much of my history, and found that we had, unknowingly, operated in some of the same areas at nearly the same time. His enterprises were, however of different sorts to mine, and we never crossed paths. As I told him how I had lost my leg, he moaned and shook his head and let a real tear fall from his eye. I was quite affected by his show of comradeship and sympathy, the first that I had encountered since my dreadful accident.

I asked him, of course, how he had lost his leg.

'Well, brother – and we are brothers indeed in this – my tale ain't as tragic as yours. I was, as I've said, in the brandy trade – 'importing' it as you will understand. I would stand ready with some business partners in the cove – ye won't mind, I'm sure, if I am sensitive about naming which one – to receive a shipment due at midnight from Roskoff. Prime French stuff it were, too. Makes me thirsty just to think of it, now.

'We was, on this partic'lar night, just after sighting their light – they had a bull's-eye in the boat's prow and signaled us with – well – I won't bore you with that detail – and we made ready to catch their painter and haul them ashore. Sudden-like comes a noise like thunder! Seems some over-zeelus Customs and Excise man had got for hisself a four-pounder, mounted on a cart, and had been aiming it right at the bull's-eye as soon as he seed it. Well, this lummox knew as much about artillery as I know about goat-herdin' in Zanzeebar, and so, when he set it off, he blowed hisself to smithereens! Not much comfort to me, I suppose, as a piece of the cart came sizzlin' through the night right at me. Struck me square in the left leg and fetched it off before you could say knife.

'Luckily some of his men had already snuck down toward the beach where we was and were able to save me from bleedin' to death. But here I is, as there you are, without a propur pair of legs between us, but two right 'uns!'

I put out my hand and he took it. We looked each other in the eye and formed a bond of one-legged brothers against the world. Or so I thought.

We spent much time together after that. Sometimes we would play a game of switching clothes and pretending to be each other at turn-out. It confused the guards no end and gave us many minutes of merriment. We learned (I thought) to trust each other, and exchanged secrets, including the locations of the caches in which we had secreted our plunder.

We vowed that when the first one of us was released, he would gather up all of the goods in both of our caches and take them to a safe place we arranged, to be divided later, when the other was released. I was grateful to have found such a good friend, who understood me, and whom I understood. We became even more like brothers in the following weeks.

I learned, sometime later, that I was soon to be freed. The London Lawyer's magic, together with some of Father's money, had gotten me clemency. I hurried to tell John.

I found him in an abstracted mood but told him my news. 'Aye, that's cheerful tidings, and I'm in need of such. My friend, I've told you of my caches, and we've vowed on our lives to help each other, but you'd better take my goods and money that you find and enjoy them yourself. I've just found that a new charge has been added to my name, with powerful evidence and witnesses, and it's sure that it's the rope for me. I'll never see the outside of Bodmin Gaol in this life.'

I was shocked, and we sat and wept together for some moments. He explained the matter further to me and I could see that he was right. He would surely hang.

'Is there anyone' I asked, 'to whom I should give your take? You've mentioned no wife nor family. What should I do?'

'Naw – there's nobody but yerself. Take it and be happy.'

The day came for my release. I was to be among others in going out of that place that day, and they brought us all into the enclosed yard to wait for the roll call and the waggon to freedom. John went with me, and we waited, within earshot of the guard who would call the roll of freedom, by the tree we had sat beneath so often.

We didn't speak. The moment was too poignant for that. I saw that a man with a paper in his hand had stepped up onto a box and soon he began to call out the names of those to be released. One by one they moved quickly toward the waiting cart which would take them through the iron gate and to freedom.

Then the thrilling moment arrived. He called my name! The next moment was not as thrilling. I felt a tremendous blow at the back of my neck, and as I lost consciousness and slumped behind the tree, I heard John Kneebone shout 'Here!'

I wasn't found, behind the tree, for several hours. It took several more to convince them that I wasn't Kneebone, but myself. Damn our play-acting and foolery!

I was let go in due course, but no-one ever saw Kneebone again. As the cart had turned the corner outside the prison-gate he had slipped off. No guards were there, of course – the other men on the cart were free men and he was taken for one, too – and the driver was half-blind and all-deaf.

Kneebone was never seen in Cornwall again. What became of him after, I don't know. I just know that our paths had better never cross again. I'll take his life for sure, but first, I'll take his other leg!

Conclusion
(Mr. Wearne Resumes)

I saw Kneebone less and less as time went by. I thought that perhaps as he left his thirties and grew into more advanced levels of skullduggery his field of endeavour may have widened and he graced other gaols, or he had been transported.

His two sons were not yet men, but seemed to be made in their father's mold, especially in height. They both were nearly six feet tall, and formidable of brawn and strength. Their poor mother, however, was not strong. How she had survived as far as she did, considering the poverty and great unhealthiness of her existence, even (perhaps especially) when Kneebone was not incarcerated, was a mystery to me. At last, however, at a time when Kneebone was absent but not in gaol, I was summoned one night to the workhouse to visit her in her final hour.

The Doctor was there, and he had done his best for her. The Vicar mumbled his prayers and turned the pages in his book. The two boys stood sentry at the head of the bed, stern and silent. Mrs. Kneebone (whose Christian name was Alice) lay pale and mottled on the straw-covered pallet. Candles flickered and seemed to intensify the darkness. Her breath came in short gasps, and soon she gasped her last.

The sons exchanged a glance and picked up some small bags and a box which I assumed to be her effects. And why not – they being her sons? They said nothing, just strode out the door, banging it after them. They were never seen again.

I arranged for her remains to be collected the next day and ordered her burial in a beggar's section of the churchyard. An unmarked depression in the ground is all that testifies to her life.

Not long thereafter I realized that I had not seen or heard news of John Kneebone in perhaps a year. Rumours, of course, floated about. One held that his body had been seen swinging from a rope in York, another held that his head was on a pike on London Bridge. Some said he had gone to sea in actual fact, not just in fancy. All nonsense, of course, but still, with a character whose imagination had been his hallmark, imagination would be applied to legends concerning him.

My life and duties went on as always. My business ventures prospered. As my enterprises concerned largely the transport of goods and the underwriting of same, I was often in ports, from tiny fishing villages like Mousehole to mighty harbors like Bristol. It was in Bristol, in fact, that I had my last glimpse of John Kneebone, although not under that name.

I was in Bristol on business several years after the sad death of Mrs. Kneebone, and was, per my custom, seeing people on the wharf and dockside. I had called on several sea-captains on their ships, money-lenders in their counting houses, brokers and dealers of divers sorts and had had a busy day of managing my affairs. It was darkening into evening, and a warm July one at that, as I trudged, full of my own thoughts, up from the waterside to where I was lodging. As I passed a public-house, I heard through the window a familiar voice.

I say familiar, but at the same time it was strange. I stopped and peered in the window. I quickly dodged to be in the shadows, as I recognized the source of the voice. I could still see in, without risk of being seen. The voice, now loud, now cajoling, now filled with hilarity as I remembered it, was from an almost unrecognizable source. Were it not for the very familiar missing left leg, I might have passed the whole thing off as coincidence, but there he was. John Kneebone in his glory.

Kneebone it was indeed, but changed almost utterly. His skin was darkly sunburnt and his forearms where they jutted from a muslin blouse were covered with tattoos. I was not close enough to discern their subject matter, but I would have wagered that they were of a sailor's design.

Another unexpected aspect of his appearance was a sailcloth apron. I saw it plainly as he swung on his crutch through the crowd of rowdy drinkers – seemingly seamen all – and roared jokes, sang snatches of song, boxed ears and played the hale-fellow to a 'T,' with a nautical flavor and a seaman's vocabulary. As he reached the end of the room, he raised a section of the bar, passed behind, and rested his forearms on the rough surface with the complaisance of a successful landlord. It was his pub, one could be sure. I passed quickly on, not wanting to be spotted, shadows or no. I had no desire to become involved with that crowd, that pub, or that landlord!

The next day, as I called on my business contacts and a few personal friends in that great city, I made casual inquiries about that pub and its publican. My first surprise is that the owner, the worthy I saw in his glory and in his apron, was not known there as 'Kneebone.'

It seemed that the rumors of his having gone to sea were true, and, furthermore, it was said and commonly believed that he had turned to piracy with a great captain of pirates and his bloodthirsty crew! In that process, he changed his surname from 'Kneebone' to – well – best not to say, for reasons to be revealed.

It was further rumoured that he was very rich, with banking accounts in all of the major cities of England and many abroad. His wife, a woman of colour, was rumored to be an African Princess of a tribe of cannibals. I made no attempt to make contact with Kneebone (as I will continue to call him.) In fact, that brief glimpse of him in his new, piratical persona was the last I ever set eyes on him in this life.

But not the last I ever heard of him. One day several years later, while visiting a town in Cornwall (to remain unnamed here) which was a center of commerce in which I had many contacts, I met a Squire of the area (a man with an admirably Cornish name, by the way.) He was a fine, talkative, open-hearted fellow. So much so I wondered that he had held onto his fortune as well as he had.

He bought drinks for everyone who so much as saluted him, and, in our conversation, revealed many pieces of what ought to have been secret business intelligence which, were I not a scrupulous man, I could have used much to my betterment and to his detriment. Such matters, it seemed, had little interest for him, and I assumed that he must somehow be much richer than his somewhat threadbare finery indicated. Indeed, I knew his house by sight, and it was of no great account from the outside.

As we sat and chatted, we were joined by a somewhat younger and 'squarer' man, a Doctor by profession. The two seemed to be quite intimate friends, and I was on the verge of excusing myself so as to allow them to converse freely when the Squire invited the Doctor and myself to his house for supper. I was delighted to go, having spent a very enjoyable time with the Squire, and as far as the Doctor, well – 'Any friend of the Squire's…' as they say.

We dined well at the Squire's table and retired to the Squire's 'growlery' for brandy and a 'touch pipe'. When there, I noticed that much of the décor, and many of the bric-a-brac in the room were of a seafaring sort. I remarked on that, and as the conversation turned in that direction, I mentioned my long-ago last glimpse of Kneebone in his public-house in Bristol. The Squire and Doctor were most fascinated by my accounts of Kneebone's early life and crimes and asked many questions.

At last the Squire and the Doctor fell silent and exchanged a look of deepest conspiracy. The Squire pledged me to secrecy as the Doctor opened a long, narrow box which lay atop a sea-chest in the corner.

The Doctor unrolled upon the table the parchment that the box had held. It looked to be a map. In the next two hours, as we switched from brandy to Navy rum, I heard a tale which sent shivers up my spine and which still inspires nightmares, and in which my old friend John featured in unexpected and fearful ways.

But I was pledged to secrecy, so that will remain a tale for another time, and another pen.

Afterword

<u>The Tales of John Kneebone</u> is a collaboration and a compilation. It began with an idea I had (I stole) from an old pamphlet; 'Two Cornish Parishes (Wendron and Sithney) In the 18th Century' by Rev. Gilbert H. Doble, M.A., Vicar of Wendron.

In it appeared our oddly-matched heroes, the two Johns, Wearne and Kneebone. They were real people who probably deserved much better than to be dragged into this book. But here they are.

It seems likely that John Wearne was some sort of shirt-tail relation of mine. Not from my immediate branch of the family, though, but likely from the branch that produced, for one, the Mayor of Helston in 1860.

The idea was to have John K. relate, to varying audiences, varying tales of how he lost his leg, tales tailored to his audience with an eye of wheedling out of them drink or coin. John W. would be the recorder of those tales.

I quailed at the idea of writing all of those stories myself, and so, in true John Kneebone fashion, I contrived a way to get others to do it for me. I am honored that so many of the best and brightest of Cornwall and elsewhere took me up on it and contributed.

The running narrative which takes us into and out of the book and the stories is all down to me. The bit of a twist at the end (which may escape readers who are not up on their swashbucklers) was my idea as well and for it I accept full blame.

I (we) hope that you have enjoyed this book and will dip into it again and again and re-read your favorites (Sorry – 'favourites' – my American roots are showing.) I feel obliged to point out that it makes a wonderful gift. I'm sure that you can think of several people who would love to have a copy.

Part, also, of the idea was to present a picture of Cornwall in the old days. The Cornish were great storytellers (still are) as well as being fine fishermen, great farmers and the best miners in the world. Those already familiar with Cornwall will, I hope, find this an affectionate, respectful and hopefully historically accurate (for the most part) reminiscence of a great age in Cornwall.

Those for whom this is a first exposure to Cornwall and the Cornish; Welcome, and please continue to learn more about the Duchy (the Nation!) of Cornwall and the great Cornish people, past and present.

At the very least, this may, I hope, provide an antidote to the distorted and unfortunate images of Cornwall that have become prevalent in modern popular culture and in the media.

Here's a list of the authors. In most of the stories, I added bits onto the beginning and end to link them to the narrative and made internal changes for consistency, but the stories are the products of the authors' fertile imaginations.

The Authors

Mike O'Connor:
A well-known Cornish-based folklorist, musicologist and bard of Gorsedh Kernow. He is the author of several books of Cornish folktales, discoverer of numerous early manuscripts of Cornish music, and adviser on Cornish music for the TV series 'Poldark'.

Craig Weatherhill:
Born 1950. Prolific Cornish author, archaeologist, historian, musician and former horseman. Bard 'Delyner Hendhyscans' (Draughtsman of Archaeology) of the Cornish Gorsedh.

Taran Spalding-Jenkin:
A spoken word poet and storyteller, known to some as 'The Cornish Writer'. He brings a little part of Cornwall with him wherever he goes, performing and running workshops across the UK on the subjects of identity, mental health and hireth.

Jim Wearne:
Cousin Jack, Author, Songwriter, Bard of Gorsedh Kernow and
originator of this book.

Kathy Wallis:
A singer, storyteller and keeper of traditions. Living in a rambling old
farmhouse on Bodmin Moor which was once the Dower House for the
Manor of Rillaton, when not looking after her cats, hens and bees, she
keeps the local traditions of Wassailing and the Crying of the Neck alive
in her hamlet.

Merv Davey:
An itinerant bagpiper and a member of the Bodmin Ragadazio who
provided the inspiration for the characters in "Pibrek". He is past Grand
Bard of Gorsedh Kernow, was awarded a PhD following his research
into Cornish folk song and dance at the institute of Cornish studies and
is the author of a series of papers and publications on Cornish folk
tradition.

Lissa Fisher:
A rather ordinary American with no penchant for the dramatic, who is an
able liar herself but will on occasion capture them on paper and try to
put them to good use.

Brian Treglown:
A Cornishman by way of Northern Michigan and Chicago. He's an
occasional writer with a penchant for Gilbert & Sullivan.

Fiona Siobhan Powell:
Tradition Bearer working in the folkways of Wales, Cornwall and the
West Country.

Nigel Pengelly:
A former farmer, turned journalist and previous editor of Cornish World. He lives in Penzance, where he was born, and now runs a media company.

Alex Langstone:
A folklore researcher and author based in Cornwall. He is editor of 'Lien Gwerin: a journal of Cornish Folklore' and has written several books, including 'From Granite to Sea - the folklore of Bodmin Moor and East Cornwall' and 'Menhir: a poetic invocation of the Cornish Landscape'. He has been interested in the folklore, legends and mysteries of the British landscape for most of his life, and lives in the Camel Valley, North Cornwall.

Matt Blewett:
Cornish born and bred. He blawed in Lanner band and survived Redruth School. Today he is treasurer for Agan Tavas, Chair of Kernow Matters To Us, President of the University students' Cornish society, dancer with Hevva, researcher, genealogist and archaeologist. In his spare time he works on a PhD about Cornish heritage, identity and democracy.

Sue Ellery-Hill:
Born in Penzance in Cornwall to Brenda and John Wootton, she grew up with strong Cornish roots and influences. After a life spent mostly involved with children's charities, she has returned to creative writing in recent years. In 2018 she was awarded two medals for Creative Writing in English by Gorsedh Kernow. She is loving living in St Just with husband Chris.

Esther Johns (Illustrator and cover design):
Artist, Cornish Speaker and Teacher. Activist and staunch supporter of Cornish rights and self-determination.